I0537974

THE GEMINI RISING ROCKIN' MACHINE

SUNSHINE DEALER MEETS THUNDER LOVE

Sunshine Dealer Meets Thunder Love
Featuring Books
Book Nine: Sunshine Dealer
Book Ten: Thunder Love
Featuring Stories
Deja-Vu
I May Never Be Able To Go Home Again

Copyright 2016 by The Gemini Rising Rockin' Machine
ISBN-13: 978-0692751954 (Gemini Rising Rockin'
Machine,The)
ISBN-10: 0692751955

The characters and events described in this book are
fictional. Any resemblance between the characters and
any person including their names, living or dead, is
purely coincidental. Because of the mature themes presented
within, reader discretion is advised.

For questions, comments you may send correspondence to.

thegeminirisingrockinmachine@twc.com

Official Website_
www.thegeminirisingrockinmachine.com

(Sunshine Dealer Meets Thunder Love)

Little By Little (Carrie And Andy)

(CARRIE)
Andy – We're so New-Together
I-Don't-Even-Know – Your-Favorite-Color

(ANDY)
Carrie– Taking-Our-Time is Kinda-Cool
But-My-Need – Is-Too-Great – To-Wait

(CARRIE)
Andy – Our-Infatuations – Are-Blooming
It's-All-About-Passion – Right-Now
My-Wants – My-Needs – Are-Pulling-Me-Closer
Making-Me – Want to Lose-Control

(ANDY)
Carrie – I If-You-Ask-My-Heart
It-Would – Tell-You-This
I-Will-Fall – In-Love-With-You
The-Fist-Time – We-Make-Love

(Chorus)
(TOGETHER) Little by Little / **(CARRIE)** Let's Take Our Time
(TOGETHER) Little by Little / **(ANDY)** Let's See What Happens
(TOGETHER) Little by Little / **(CARRIE)** Maybe We'll Fall In Love
(TOGETHER) Little by Little / **(TOGETHER)** For The Rest Of Our Lives

(CARRIE)
Andy – You're-What-I-Want – In a Man
Regretfully – I-Have-This-Feeling – That-You'll-Take
Then-Leave – Making-Me-Regret
That-I-Gave-You – What-You-Wanted
Instead of Waiting – 'Til-You-Loved-Me

(Chorus)
(TOGETHER) Little by Little / **(CARRIE)** Let's Take Our Time
(TOGETHER) Little by Little / **(ANDY)** Let's See What Happens
(TOGETHER) Little by Little / **(CARRIE)** Maybe We'll Fall In Love
(TOGETHER) Little by Little / **(TOGETHER)** For The Rest Of Our Lives

(ANDY)
Carrie – Love is a Chance
I-Want-It – I-Think-I-Need-It
But-I-Can't-Wait – Much-Longer

Carrie – I-Can't – Give-My-Heart to You
Until-I-Have a Taste – Of-Your-Flame
That-Way – I-Will-Know
Our-Love – Won't-Burn-Away

(Chorus)
(TOGETHER) Little by Little / (CARRIE) Let's Take Our Time
(TOGETHER) Little by Little / (ANDY) Let's See What Happens
(TOGETHER) Little by Little / (CARRIE) Maybe We'll Fall In Love
(TOGETHER) Little by Little / (TOGETHER) For The Rest Of Our Lives

(CARRIE)
Andy – We're so New-Together
I-Don't-Even-Know – Your-Favorite-Color

(ANDY)
Carrie– Taking-Our-Time is Kinda-Cool
But-My-Need – Is-Too-Great – To-Wait

(CARRIE)
Andy – Our-Infatuations – Are-Blooming
It's-All-About-Passion – Right-Now

(ANDY)
Carrie – I-Will-Fall – In-Love-With-You
The-Fist-Time – We-Make-Love

(CARRIE) Andy – You're-What-I-Want – In a Man

(ANDY) Carrie – Love is a Chance

(Chorus)
(TOGETHER) Little by Little / (CARRIE) Let's Take Our Time
(TOGETHER) Little by Little / (ANDY) Let's See What Happens
(TOGETHER) Little by Little / (CARRIE) Maybe We'll Fall In Love
(TOGETHER) Little by Little / (TOGETHER) For The Rest Of Our Lives

Book Nine: Sunshine Dealer (Pages 4-34)
(The Numbers after the Song Titles are the Original Numbering. Every Song in this Book is a **New Song** Written for this Book, minus the B's)

(Side One)
161. Sunshine Dealer (606.)
    Sunshine Lover **(928.)**
162. Sunshine And You (142 Songs Later) (611.)
    Sunshine And You (Original Version) (469.) **(Bonus)**
163. Shine Down On Me (612.)
164. Let My Love Shine Down On You (613.)
165. Sun Shining Love (614.)
    I'm A Sun Lover **(930.)**

(Side Two)
166. Love Is Slow (615.)
167. I'm Back In The Love Groove (616.)
168. Love Is A Battle (617.)
    Love is The Word **(931.)**
169. You're Everything I Always Wanted (618.)
    Everything To Me **(932.)**
170. Lovin' In The Sun (623.)

(Side Three)
171. Take My Heart (624.)
172. Fine Love (625.)
    Fine Love Maker **(933.)**
173. Full Moon Heart (641.)
174. Fly With Me (642.)
175. In The Beat Of A Heart (643.)

(Side Four)
176. The Tidal Wave Of Love (644.)
177. Refund On Love (645.)
    I'm Refunding Your Love **(934.)**
178. Soak In The Sun (646.)
179. The Last Day Of Summer (647.)
180. Dead Of Winter (648.)

(Bonus Songs)
She Wants To Be Loved (359.) / Do You Love Me Baby (391.)

161. Sunshine Dealer

All-My-Love
For-You – My-Darling
So-Thankful – For-Your-Love
For-You-Showed-Me – The-True-Meaning
Of-What – Real-Love is All-About

I-Feel – So-Good
I-Have-It – So-Great
Feeling the Peace of Your-Love
Basking in It – Every-Single-Day
Never a Sad-Thought
Going-Through – My-Mind

(Chorus)
You Must Be A Sunshine Dealer
Or-Work-Hand-In-Hand-With-The-Sun
For You Shine So Bright
That You Radiate – Your
Sweet-Shining-Beautiful-Love

All-My-Love
For-You – My-Darling
So-Thankful – For-Your-Love
For-You-Showed-Me – The-True-Meaning
Of-What – Real-Love is All-About

I-Feel – So-Good
I-Have-It – So-Great
Feeling the Peace of Your-Love
Basking in It – Every-Single-Day
Never a Sad-Thought
Going-Through – My-Mind

(Chorus)
You Must Be A Sunshine Dealer
Or-Work-Hand-In-Hand-With-The-Sun
For You Shine So Bright
That You Radiate – Your
Sweet-Shining-Beautiful-Love

Sunshine Lover

My-Love is Flickering
I'm-Up – I'm-Down
I-Need a Date – Before-I – Shake-Away
Better-Check the Want-Adds
Before-Mr.-Happy – Becomes-Mr.-Sad

Do-You-Need-Love / Yes-I-Do
Do-You-Live-In-Town / Yes-I-Do
Do-You-Have a Great-Job / Yes-I-Do
Then-Give-Me a Call / I-Think-I-Will – Right-Now

(Chorus)
Hello Sunshine Lover
Here I Am – Ready To Go
Sunshine Lover
I Love What You're – Hardly Wearing
Sunshine Lover
You're My Favorite Lover
Sunshine Lover
What Do You Mean – My Time Is Up

My-Love is Flickering
I'm-Up – I'm-Down
I-Need a Date – Before-I – Shake to Pieces
Better-Check – Who's-Free-Tonight
Before-Mr.-Happy – Becomes-Mr.-Sad

Do-You-Need-Love / Yes-I-Do
Do-You-Live-In-Town / Yes-I-Do
Do-You-Have a Great-Job / Yes-I-Do
Then-Give-Me a Call / I-Think-I-Will – Right-Now

(Chorus)
Hello Sunshine Lover
Here I Am – Ready To Go
Sunshine Lover
I Love What You're – Hardly Wearing
Sunshine Lover
You're My Favorite Lover
Sunshine Lover
What Do You Mean – My Time Is Up

162. Sunshine And You (142 Songs Later)

Good-Morning – My-Love
It's-Such a Beautiful Day
The-Sun is Shining so Bright
Just-Like – Your-Lovely-Heart

Beautiful oh Beautiful
I-Want to Hold and Kiss
Make-Love to You
You're-My-Everything
Let's-Share – Our-Love
Start-Our-Day-Lovin' – Just-Right

(Chorus)
Sunshine And You
In My Life Is A Paradise
That I Enjoy With Such Delight
Never Having To Worry About
Any Stormy Weather

Good-Evening – My-Love
I-Missed-You so Much
My-Day – Was-Long – And a Drag
I'm so Happy – The-Night-Has-Fallen
So-I-Can-Be – With-You – My-Love

It's so Nice and Peaceful
Knowing – Our-Love for Each-Other
Is-Just-Like-This – Sunny-Day-Was
Wonderful and Warm
The-Always-Welcoming
Home-Sweet – Loving-Home

(Chorus)
Sunshine And You
In My Life Is A Paradise
That I Enjoy With Such Delight
Never Having To Worry About
Any Stormy Weather

Sunshine And You (Original Version) (Bonus)

This-Is the Most-Sweet
Mind-Rockin'-Song
I-Will – Ever-Write
It's-Titled so Nicely
Sunshine and You
It's-Just-For-You
The Everybody and The-Anybody

Alright – Are-You-Ready
Clap – Your – Hands
Tap – Your – Feet
We're-Going to Have
Such a Great-Time
Ready – Here-We-Go

(Chorus)
Sunshine And You
In My Life
Is Like A Paradise
That I Can Enjoy
Never Having To Worry
About Any Stormy Weather

What-Do-You-Think
About this Song so far
What's-That – You-Say
Not-Mushy – Enough-For-You
Well – Here-You-Go-Then
Remember – You-Asked-For-This

(Chorus)
Sunshine And You
In My Life
Is Like A Paradise
That I Can Enjoy
Never Having To Worry
About Any Stormy Weather

Sunshine and You
Oh-What a Beautiful-Day
I-Pick-Out a Pretty-Flower
Place-It in Your-Hair
I-Take-Your-Hand – Placing-It – In-Mine
Feeling-Your – Soft-Skin

I-Kiss-Your – Sweet-Hand
For the Sweet-Lady – That-You-Are
Whispering to Myself
That-I-Would-Love – Just to Kiss-You

But-You're-Such a Lady – I'm-Not-Worthy
So-I-Keep-My-Love – For-You to Myself
And-Place – Your-Face – In-My-Dreams

(Chorus)
Sunshine And You
In My Life
Is Like A Paradise
That I Can Enjoy
Never Having To Worry
About Any Stormy Weather

Well – What-Do-You – Think-Now
How-This-Song – Turned-Out
I-Don't-Know – About-All of You
But-I-Think – I-Better-Stop-Now
Because – I'm-Starting to Love-Itch – All-Over

(Chorus)
Sunshine And You
In My Life
Is Like A Paradise
That I Can Enjoy
Never Having To Worry
About Any Stormy Weather

Just-Kidding – Love-Rules
Oh-Yes-It-Does – Sing-It-With-Me
Love-Rules – Love-Rules – Love-Rules
We-Ain't-No-Fools – Because – Love-Rules
Now-Everybody – Give-Yourself a Hug
Not-Too-Tight – Just-Loving-Right
9

163. Shine Down On Me

Lost-In a World of Sadness
My-Love-Is so Very-Scarred
I-Give-My – Heart-Up
Too-Easy – Too-Fast

Love-Hurts – I-Know
I-Accept-This – Because-I'm-Lonely
In the Need of Some-Love – From-Someone
Like-Me – Someone – That is Scarred

(Pre-Chorus)
I Cry For The Day – I Cry For My Hurting Heart
Icy Chills In My Veins – Makes Me Plead For Help

(Chorus)
Shine Down On Me
Warm – Beautiful Sun
My Love Feels Like
It's Frozen Inside Me
Shine Down On Me
Warm – Beautiful Sun
Set Me Free – From My Pain

Summer is Fading-Away – Fall is Settling-In
I'm-All-Alone – Once-Again
Preparing-Myself – For the Coldness
Of a Long and Freezing-Winter
Waking-Up – To the Sun – Shining-On-My-Face
Maybe-Today – Will-Be-My-Day for Love

(Pre-Chorus)
I Cry For The Day – I Cry For My Hurting Heart
Icy Chills In My Veins – Makes Me Plead For Help

(Chorus)
Shine Down On Me
Warm – Beautiful Sun
My Love Feels Like
It's Frozen Inside Me
Shine Down On Me
Warm – Beautiful Sun
Set Me Free – From My Pain

164. Let My Love Shine Down On You

Broken-Lover – Reach-Out
I'm-Here for You
I-Have a Lot of Love
To-Help – You-Mend
Your – Broken – Heart

Let-Me-Be a Healing-Hand
That-Allows-You – The-Chance
To-Dry – Your-Tears
Take-Away – Your-Fears
So-You-Can-Be – Free to Fly-Free
Soaring-Towards a New-Love

(Chorus)
Let My Love Shine Down On You
I Love You So Much
Let My Love Shine Down On You
I Want You To Love Me
As Much As I Love You

Can-You-Feel-Me
My-Touch – My-Warmth
Look-Into – My-Eyes
Trust-What-You-See
I-Love-You – I-Always-Have

We've-Been-Friends – For so Long
I-Know-You – Love-Me-As a Friend
With-My-Heart – In-My-Hands
I-Want-You to Love-Me – Like a Lover
That-Will-Be-Here – For-You
Loving-You – Forever and Ever

(Chorus)
Let My Love Shine Down On You
I Love You So Much
Let My Love Shine Down On You
I Want You To Love Me
As Much As I Love You

165. Sun Shining Love

Heading-Out-My-Door – Ready
Don't-Want to Be-Late
'Cause-I-Have – Another-Hot-Date
With-This – Hot-Lovely-Lady

This-Lady – Has-Been – On-My-Mind
Ever-Since – I-Saw-Her – From-Behind
Bathing-Naked – In the Sun
My-Eyes – Could-Not-Look-Away
From-Her – Beautiful-Bare-Body

(Chorus)
Sun Shining Love
I Want You So Much
I'll Do Anything You Need
Just To Be Able To Enjoy Your
Sun Shining Love For Awhile

With-No-Fear
She-Looks-Me – In-My-Eyes
Pointing – Telling-Me
That-Her-Eyes – Are-Up-Here
Loving the Excitement – She-Brings
Knowing – I-Want-Some-Lovin'

She's-In – Total-Control
Making-Me – Beg so Hard
Just to Keep – Touching
'Cause – She's so Fine
She – Knows – This
Which is Very – Very-Fine
For a Lonely-Man – Like-Me

(Chorus)
Sun Shining Love
I Want You So Much
I'll Do Anything You Need
Just To Be Able To Enjoy Your
Sun Shining Love For Awhile

I'm A Sun Lover

I-Live-With a Smile
I-Live-With – Pain
Yesterday-Was – Warm and Sunny
Today – It's-Raining-Down-Hard

Tomorrow – I-Don't-Know
What-Will-Come – To-Be
But-Inside-My-Soul
I-Will-Let – The-Sun-Shine

(Chorus)
Hello Love – I'm Single
I'm A Sun Lover
That's What I Am
Would You Like To Play With Me
Hello Love – I'm Single
I'm A Sun Lover
That's What I Am
Would You Like To Play With Me

I-Get-Up – I-Fall-Down
Life-Is-Great – Life-Sucks
Heaven and Hell – Rainbows and Icy-Storms
My-Heart – Will-Not-Melt
My-Heart – Will-Not-Freeze

Gray-Skies – With-No-Clouds
It's-Such an Ugly-Day
Lovers-Next to Me – Are-Laughing
Blink-My-Eyes – I-See a New-Love – Coming-My-Way
Inside-My-Soul – The-Sun is Still-Shining

(Chorus)
Hello Love – I'm Single
I'm A Sun Lover
That's What I Am
Would You Like To Play With Me
Hello Love – I'm Single
I'm A Sun Lover
That's What I Am
Would You Like To Play With Me

166. Love Is Slow

The-Past – Was-Not a Blast
When-You-Left – Your-Lonely-Home
Looking – For-Some-Love
Only to Find – More-Loneliness

Alone-In-This-World
You-Still – Search for Love
Your-Fire – Burns-Strong
But-Your – Sad-Heart
Makes – Your – Eyes
Cry-Out – Your-Lonely-Pain

(Chorus)
Love Is Slow – When You're Lonely
It's A Leap Of Faith – For Your Re-Breaking Heart
Love Is Slow – When You Need It The Most
Love Is Slow – It 's Never On Time
Love Is Slow – Even When You're Full Of Love
It's A Leap Of Faith – For Your Re-Breaking Heart
Be Patient – One Day – Love Will Be Yours

In the Dark – You're-All-Alone
Once-Again – Wanting-Love
Not – Another-Night of
I'll-Call-You – Tomorrow
I Promise

Wanting to Be-Touched
Makes-You – Say-Yes
As-You-Blindly – Close-Your-Eyes
Pretending – It's-Love – Even-If
It-Only-Lasts – For a Few
Moments of Time

(Chorus)
Love Is Slow – When You're Lonely
It's A Leap Of Faith – For Your Re-Breaking Heart
Love Is Slow – When You Need It The Most
Love Is Slow – It 's Never On Time
Love Is Slow – Even When You're Full Of Love
It's A Leap Of Faith – For Your Re-Breaking Heart
Be Patient – One Day – Love Will Be Yours

167. I'm Back In The Love Groove

Taking – My – Time
On-Slow – Running-Love
Was the Way – I-Was
But-Not-Anymore – No-Way

I-Want to Feel – Good
I-Want to Be – In-Love
Like-I-Use to Be
When-I-Was – In a Love-Groove

(Chorus)
Rockets In The Air
I'm Back In The Love Groove
It's Way Out Of Sight
It's Filled With Such Delight
I'm Back – I'm Back
In The Love Groove
Come Love Groove With Me

Darling – Oh-Darling
You're-So-Fine
I-Need – Some-Lovin'
I-Want to Feel – Its Groove

I-Can-Give-Back so Good
The-Love – You-Need so Bad
Take-My-Hand – Lick-My-Tongue
Let's-Find-Our – Love-Groove

(Chorus)
Rockets In The Air
I'm Back In The Love Groove
It's Way Out Of Sight
I'm Filled With Such Delight
I'm Back – I'm Back
In The Love Groove

168. Love Is A Battle

Lost-Roaming in My-Mind
I-Try to Forget the Pain
But its Memory is Too-Clear
To-Let-Me-Feel – Any-Peace

All-I-Can-Do is Suffer-On
One-Day – At a Time
Building-Up – My-Love-Strength
'Til it's Strong-Enough
To-Flow – Free and Fine

(Chorus)
Love Is A Battle
I'm Always On The Losing Side
I Try To Keep The Peace
Making Them Feel Loved
Until I'm All Alone
Healing From My Love Scars

The-Spark – In-My-Heart
Helps-Me – Survive-My – Heartbreaks
Even-Though – I-Feel-Them
All the Way – To-My-Soul

Being in Love – Is-Priceless
Loneliness – Tears at Me
With-Time and Some-Hope
Love-Can – Come-Up to Me
Taking-Away – All-My-Loneliness

(Chorus)
Love Is A Battle
I'm Always On The Losing Side
I Try To Keep The Peace
Making Them Feel Loved
Until I'm All Alone
Healing From My Love Scars

Love is The Word

I-Walk-Free – Kiss the Sky
I'm-In-Love – Lick the Moon
Pains of Yesterday – I-Gave the Boot
Hating-World – Take a Chill-Pill
If-You-Don't-Know – Love-Is-The-Word

(Chorus)
What Is The Word – Love Is The Word
That's Right – Love Is The Word
When Everything Is Great
Love Is The Word
When Everything Goes Bad

Love Is The Word
When You're In Love
Love Is The Word
When You're Heartbroken
Love Is The Word
Before – During And After The War

I-Walk-Free – Kiss the Sky
I'm-In-Love – Lick the Moon
Pains of Yesterday – I-Gave the Boot
Hating-World – Take a Chill-Pill
If-You-Don't-Know – Love-Is-The-Word

(Chorus)
What Is The Word – Love Is The Word
That's Right – Love Is The Word
When Everything Is Great
Love Is The Word
When Everything Goes Bad

Love Is The Word
When You're In Love
Love Is The Word
When You're Heartbroken
Love Is The Word
Before – During – And After – The War

169. You're Everything I Always Wanted

Love is Alive – In-Me
I-Met-This – Fine-Love
That-Took-Away – All-My-Blues
Leaving-My – Heart and Soul
Feeling-Fresh and New
Like-They-Did – When-I-Was-Young

(Chorus)
You're Everything I Always Wanted
I Love You So Much
You're Everything I Always Wanted
You Love Me So Much
I'm Everything You Always Wanted
Let's Love Each Other Forever

When-You're in Love
Life-Is so Fine and Right
With-No-Tears – In-Your-Eyes
No-Rips in Your-Heart
To-Keep-You – All-By-Yourself
Without – Someone to Love

(Chorus)
You're Everything I Always Wanted
I Love You So Much
You're Everything I Always Wanted
You Love Me So Much
I'm Everything You Always Wanted
Let's Love Each Other Forever

Fine-Love – Oh-Baby – Fine-Love
You-Are – So-Special
You're-Everything – I-Always-Wanted
Wrapped so Nicely and Sweet
Inside the Most – Perfect-Body
I've-Ever – Made-Love-To

(Repeat Chorus)

Everything To Me

It's-Five-O' Clock – Work-Day is Finally-Over
It's-Time for Love
It's-Time to Rock
Can't-Wait – Don't-Want to Be-Late

My-Baby's – Coming-Over
We're-Going to Jump-in the Sack
Then-Grab – Something to Eat
If-We – Have the Time

(Chorus)
Your-Face – Your-Heart
Your-Love – Your-Soul
Is Everything To Me
No Matter How Good
No Matter How Bad
You're Everything To Me
Baby I Love You – This Much

It's-Eight-O' Clock – Goodnight and She's-Gone
Have to Hurry – Only-Have an Hour
It's-Time for More-Lovin'
It's-Time to Rock-Harder
Can't-Wait – For-She –Won't-Be-Late

My-Baby's – Coming-Over
We're-Going to Jump-in the Sack
Then-Grab – Something to Eat
If-We-Can – Get-Out of Bed

(Chorus)
Your-Face – Your-Heart
Your-Love – Your-Soul
Is Everything To Me
No Matter How Good
No Matter How Bad
You're Everything To Me
Baby I Love You – This Much

170. Lovin' In The Sun

I-Don't – Know-Her-Name
She-Hasn't – Told-Me-Yet
And-I – Don't-Mind at All
Her-Name – Is the Last-Thing
On-My – Loving-Mind

I-Can-Tell – She-Wants to Play
With-Me – For-Awhile
Letting-Love – Stay-Away
So-She-Can – Have a Great-Time
With-Out-Any-Drama – Hanging-Around

(Chorus)
One Day At A Time
Living Her Life
She Plays It So Safe
Until She Meets Me This Day
Now We're Having Fun
Lovin' In The Sun
Like We Lust Each Other

When-The-Sun – Is-Shining-Down – So-Bright
You're-Lovin' – Feeling so Right
The-Thoughts of Being-Wrong
Seems so Far-Away and Forgotten

When-Two – Lustful-People
Like-Us – Are-Enjoying – Our-Lust
On-This-Beautiful – Warm-Summer's-Day
Wishing – Every-Day – Our-Lives
Could-Always-Be – So-Wonderfully
Free-Loving and Lusting

(Chorus)
One Day At A Time
Living Her Life
She Plays It So Safe
Until She Meets Me This Day
Now We're Having Fun
Lovin' In The Sun
Like We Lust Each Other

171. Take My Heart

Heart-Broken – On a Sunday
My-Life – Is so Sad
That-Love – Did-Not-Stay
Within – My – Heart

Instead it Drifted-Away
From-Me so Very-Fast
Love-Was-There – I-Turned-My-Head
I-Turned-It – Back-Again
Love-Was-Nowhere – To-Be-Found

(Chorus)
Take My Heart
Love Me Baby
Take My Heart
Fill It Full Of Love
Take My Heart
Love Me Baby
Take My Heart
Fill It Full Of Love

Looking at You – I-Don't-Know-You
In-Your-Eyes – I-See-My-Sadness
Wondering to Myself – If-Your-Heart
Is as Broken as Mine – On-This-Day

Sit-Beside-You – Say-Hello
Your-Sad-Eyes – Say to Me – Go-Away
I-Take-Your – Soft-Hand – Put into My
Slow-Beating – Alone-Heart
For the Both of Us
I-Sing to You – This-Song

(Chorus)
Take My Heart
Love Me Baby
Take My Heart
Fill It Full Of Love
Take My Heart
Love Me Baby
Take My Heart
Fill It Full Of Love

21

172. Fine Love

Sunday – Out in The-Sun
Running in The-Soft
Green-Grass – Of-Summer
Like-There – Is-No-Tomorrow

We're-In-Love – We-Don't-Care
What-This-World – Thinks-About-Us
Let it Have – Its Hate and Sorrow
While-We – Bask in Happiness

(Chorus)
We Have Such A Fine Love
To Love Each Other With
Too Bad This World
Won't Take A Look At Us
Seeing In Us Such A Fine Love

With-Hot – Sweaty-Sticky-Bodies
With-Grass – Stained-Feet
We-Take a Break – From-Out of The-Sun
To-Make-Love – Until-Dark
Out of Nowhere – Lightening-Strikes
Thunder-Roars – As-Rain – Begins to Fall

We- Pause a Moment – We-Smile
Saying-Out-Loud – Together as One
Not-Even – Mother Nature – In-Her-Fury
Can-Take-Away – From-Our-Memory
This-Wonderful – Summer-Day
We-Shared-Together – In-Love

(Chorus)
We Have Such A Fine Love
To Love Each Other With
Too Bad This World
Won't Take A Look At Us
Seeing In Us Such A Fine Love

Fine Love Maker

Morning – Noon and Night
I've-Had-Them – Tall
I've-Had-Them – Short
Morning – Noon and Night
I've-Had-Them – In a Bed
I've-Had-Them – In a Car

But-Sweet-Baby – You're-My-Favorite
You-Always – Come-First

(Chorus)
She's Fine – Oh Yes She Is
She's My Fine Love Maker
Making Love To Me
The Past Three Weeks
She's Fine – Oh Yes She Is
She's My Fine Love Maker
Making Love To Me
The Past Three Weeks
Here's Hoping She Goes For Four

Morning – Noon and Night
I've-Had-Them – Tall
I've-Had-Them – Short
Morning – Noon and Night
I've-Had-Them – In a Bed
I've-Had-Them – In a Car

But-Sweet-Baby – You're-My-Favorite
You-Always – Come-First

(Chorus)
She's Fine – Oh Yes She Is
She's My Fine Love Maker
Making Love To Me
The Past Three Weeks
She's Fine – Oh Yes She Is
She's My Fine Love Maker
Making Love To Me
The Past Three Weeks
Here's Hoping She Goes For Four

173. Full Moon Heart

She's-Been-Hurt by Love
It's-Cost-Her – Her-Heart
All-Her-Thoughts – About-Love
Are-Forgotten – Lost in Her-Soul
Loneliness – Breeds – Sadness
It's-In-Her-Eyes – All-See
That-She-Ignores – Without-Smiling

She-Knows – That-She's-Lying to Herself
She-Doesn't-Care – It's-Better-This-Way
She-Never-Has to Worry – If-They-Love-Her
Or – Waiting to Break – Her-Heart

(Chorus)
She's Cold As Ice
Not Looking For Love
Until The Full Moon Rises
Then Her Full Moon Heart
Rises Without Her Permission
Making Her Want To Be Loved

She-Slips – Herself into Love
A-Few-Nights a Month
Breaking-Their-Hearts – After
The-Full-Moon is Gone
Forgetting-All-About-Them
With-The-Rising – Of-The-Sun

She-Knows – That-She's-Lying to Herself
She-Doesn't-Care – It's-Better-This-Way
She-Never-Has to Worry – If-They-Love-Her
Or – Waiting to Break – Her-Heart

(Chorus)
She's Cold As Ice
Not Looking For Love
Until The Full Moon Rises
Then Her Full Moon Heart
Rises Without Her Permission
Making Her Want To Be Loved

174. Fly With Me

Friday-Night – Turned to Sorrow
As-We-Drove-Along
Both of Us – Paying-Attention
To-The-One – We-Love

Snow-Falling – So-Romantically
Slick-Spot – On the Road
We-Spun and We-Spun
Sliding – Down a Hill
To-Our-Deaths

(Chorus)
Fly With Me
Straight Out Of Our Bodies
Fate Has Been Fickle
Leaving Us Free Souls
To Roam This World
Until We Are Called Home

Floating-Above-My-Body
Looking-Down at You
Your-Soul is Scared – Stiff
I-Tell-You – Not to Fear – Our-End
For-This is Only – Our-Beginning

I-Try and I-Try – As-You-Shake – Your-Soul-No
A-Calling – From-Beyond – Enters-My-Spirit
You-Watch as Golden-Wings – Appear on My-Back
I-Flap-Them – For-You to Want
Fear-Slips-Away – As-You-Follow-Me
Winged-In-Gold – Flying-Towards-Heaven

(Chorus)
Fly With Me
Straight Out Of Our Bodies
Fate Has Been Fickle
Leaving Us Free Souls
To Roam This World
Until We Are Called Home

25

175. In The Beat Of A Heart

You've – Got-It-All
With so Much – More
I-Like to See – Your-Clothes
On-My – Bedroom-Floor

Let's-Get-Together
Let's-Head – For the Exit
Tomorrow – Will-Be a New-Day
For-Us to Say – No-To
Tonight – Let's-Just-Say – Yes

(Chorus)
In The Beat Of A Heart
We're Side By Side
In The Beat Of A Heart
We're Hot And Rockin'
In The Beat Of A Heart
No One Better Come A Knockin'

Welcome to My-Home – Love
Kick-Off – Your-Dancing-Shoes
Dance-With-Me – To-My-Bed
Sexy-Stranger – I-Just-Met
Let's-Become-Lovers – That-Melt
Loneliness to Dust

(Chorus)
In The Beat Of A Heart
We're Side By Side
In The Beat Of A Heart
We're Hot And Rockin'
In The Beat Of A Heart
No One Better Come A Knockin'

In-The-Blink of An-Eye
We-Get – Undressed
In a Whisper's – Breath
We-Want to Feel – Love
In the Beat – Of a Heart
Is-Where-We – Will-Lovingly-Stay

(Repeat Chorus)
26

176. The Tidal Wave Of Love

Do-You-Remember-Me
I-Remember-You – Pretty-Flower
The-Night – We-Shared-Together
Was a Night – Well-Spent
One-That-I – Have-Not-Forgotten

I-See in Your-Eyes
You-Remember – My-Name
The-One – That's-Been on Your
Lovin'-Lips – For so Many-Lonely
Safe and Calm – Long-Nights

(Chorus)
We Did It Once – We Can Do It Again
The Tidal Wave Of Love
We Created For Our Loneliness
We Did It Once – We Can Do It Again
The Tidal Wave Of Love
We Created – So We Can Get Laid In Peace

No-Sorrow – No-Guilt – No-Shame
Just-Two-Lovers – Not
Loved-Wrecked on This-Beautiful
Warm and Sunny – Next-Day-After

We-Don't-Wonder – What-Now
We-Know – In-Our-Hearts
That-Our-Wonderful – One of a Kind
Tidal-Wave of Love – Is a Rushing
Wave of Free – Loving-Love
That-Will-Never – Run-Out of Power

(Chorus)
We Did It Once – We Can Do It Again
The Tidal Wave Of Love
We Created For Our Loneliness
We Did It Once – We Can Do It Again
The Tidal Wave Of Love
We Created – So We Can Get Laid In Peace

177. Refund On Love

They-Say – Lonely-Lovers
Close-Their-Eyes – While-They're
Looking for Love
Gladly – Bumping into It
In-The-Dark – Of a Lonely-Night

Next-Day – Adding-Up the Cost
The-Receipt of Sex – That-Had-No
Price of Love – Printed on It
Leaving-Them – With a One-Time
Use-Only – Then-Throw-It-Away
Because-There-Is – Nothing to Return

(Chorus)
Demand All You Want
But There Is No
Refund On Love
It Is What It Is
Everything And Nothing At All
With No Refund On Love

They-Say – That-Lovers – That-Live
Together – For so Many-Years
Sometimes – Have-Their-Love
Feel to Them – Like it's Gotten-Old

They-Count-Up – The-Years
They-Spent – Getting to This-Day
With a Hard-Breath – Exhaled
They-Realize-Sadly – That-Love
Has-No-Warranties or Guarantees

(Chorus)
Demand All You Want
But There Is No
Refund On Love
It Is What It Is
Everything And Nothing At All
With No Refund On Love

I'm Refunding Your Love

I-Gave-You – My-Heart
I-Gave-You – My-Love
Then-One-Day – You-Said-Forget-Me
And-Had-Sex – With-Some-Ugly-Guy

Didn't-Know – What to Say
Didn't-Know – What to Do
'Til-I-Thought-About-It
My-Answer – Screw-You

(Chorus)
Lady Cold Lady
I'm Refunding Your Love
It's Not Worth The Price
To My Angry Heart
Lady Cold Lady
I'm Refunding Your Love
It's Not Worth The Price
To My Angry Heart
Give Me Back My Picture

I-Gave-You – My-Heart
I-Gave-You – My-Love
Then-One-Day – You-Said-Forget-Me
And-Had-Sex – With-Some-Ugly-Guy

Didn't-Know – What to Say
Didn't-Know – What to Do
'Til-I-Thought-About-It
My-Answer – Screw-You

(Chorus)
Lady Cold Lady
I'm Refunding Your Love
It's Not Worth The Price
To My Angry Heart
Lady Cold Lady
I'm Refunding Your Love
It's Not Worth The Price
To My Angry Heart
Give Me Back My Picture

178. Soak In The Sun

I-Live-My-Life – With-No-Regrets
One-Day – At a Time – Is-My-Way
I-Find-Love – I-Lose-Love
Tomorrow is Another-Day for Love
To-Come-Up to Me and Say-Hello

True-Love – Is a Nerve-Wrecking
Entity-That-I – Crave so Much
It's-Out-There – Somewhere
All-I-Got to Do – Is-Find-It
Until-Then – I'll-Just

(Chorus)
Soak In The Sun
Letting Its Warmth
Rewarm My Lonely Heart
'Til It's Hot Enough To Beat Strong
On Another Cold – Love Seeking Night

I-Live-My-Life – With-No-Regrets
One-Day – At a Time – Is-My-Way
Love-Comes and Love-Goes
So-Many-Lovers so Many-Times
Lots of Pretty-Faces – Lost-Within – My-Mind

I'm-Alright – I'm-Living-My-Life
Days-Are-Growing – Shorter-Every-Day
I-Ask-My-Heart – One-More-Time
Does-This-Fine-Lady – I-Just-Met
Have a Chance – To-Be-My – Shot at Finding
True-Love or Just-Another
Fading – Future – Ex-Lover
Until-Then – I'll-Just

(Chorus)
Soak In The Sun
Letting Its Warmth
Rewarm My Lonely Heart
'Til It's Hot Enough To Beat Strong
On Another Cold – Love Seeking Night

179. The Last Day Of Summer

Stop the Sadness – Darling
Get-Dressed in Something – Little
That-Matches – This-Sunny-Day
Something-That-Will-Not – Let-Me-Stop
Looking at You – With-Both-Eyes

Let's-Walk – On the Beach
Let's-Have-Lunch – On a Cliff
Late-Afternoon – Will-Be-High
In-The-Sky – In a Air-Balloon
When the Night – Falls
We'll-Be-Making-Love – In-The-Moon-Light

(Chorus)
Today Is a Great Day
A Day To Celebrate – A Day
To Remember – Because It's
The Last Day Of Summer
So Don't Be So Down Darling
Let's Have One More Day
Having Fun And Love In The Sun

Darling – Come-Over
Lay-Down – Beside-Me
You-Look so Sweet
I'd-Love to Feel – You-Again

Thank-You-Darling – For-Making
The-Last-Day Of Summer
Something for Me to Remember
When it Becomes – The-Dead of Winter

(Chorus)
Today Is a Great Day
A Day To Celebrate – A Day
To Remember – Because It's
The Last Day Of Summer
So Don't Be So Down Darling
Let's Have One More Day
Having Fun And Love In The Sun

31

180. Dead Of Winter

When the Sun – Begins to Fade
As the Snow – Begins to Pile-Up
Summertime is Just a Memory
For-Our-Minds to Remember
As-Our-Bodies – Shake-From the Cold

Love is Alive – In-Our-Hearts
We're-Still-Together as One
No-Matter-What – Nature-Brings-Us
We'll-Make it Through – Because
Summertime is Not – That-Far-Away

(Chorus)
The Dead Of Winter
Is Upon Us My Darling
If You Need My Warmth
Just Lay Down Next To Me
We'll Hibernate Together Until
The Sun Starts To Get Warm Again

Hard-Snow – Fell-Down – Upon-Us
As-We – Weathered the Storm
Winter's – Beautiful-Magic – Revealed
Foot-Upon-Foot of High-Mounting-Snow

That-Took the Better-Part of a Day
For-Us to Dig – Our-Freezing-Bodies
Out of Our – Winter's-Prison – To-Find a
Civilization – That-Was as Freezing as Us

(Chorus)
The Dead Of Winter
Is Upon Us My Darling
If You Need My Warmth
Just Lay Down Next To Me
We'll Hibernate Together Until
The Sun Starts To Get Warm Again

(Bonus)
She Wants To Be Loved (359.)

You're-Not-Good-Enough
To be Loved by Her
She-Deserves to Smile – Big-Time
Laughing-Away – Having-Fun
Loving – Being in Love

Not-Drowning – In-Your-Funk
But-You're so Selfish
You-Only-Think of Yourself
Not-What – She-Truly-Needs

(Chorus)
She Wants To Be Loved
If You Don't Have It
Inside Your Lost Heart
To Make Her Feel Loved
Step A Side – So I Can
Give Her All My Love
That I Know She Needs
So Very Loving Much

Because of Your-Dullness
Her-Smile is Fading-Away
Her-Special – Loving-Spark
Is-Slowly – Fading-Away

She's-Starting to Just-Stare – When
Everybody is Laughing at a Joke
It-Makes-Me so Sad – That-I-Can't
Grab-Her-Up and Show-Her
What-Love – Could-Be-Like – With-Me

(Chorus)
She Wants To Be Loved
If You Don't Have It
Inside Your Lost Heart
To Make Her Feel Loved
Step A Side – So I Can
Give Her All My Love
That I Know She Needs
So Very Loving Much
33

(Bonus)
Do You Love Me Baby (391.)

When-I – Want-Some-Lovin'
I-Reach-Out to You – But-You
Push-My-Hands-Away – Saying
Later-Baby – Not-Now-Baby

Everyone – Has the Right to Say-No
But-Baby – It's Becoming a Trend
That-I – Don't-Want-No-Part-Of
So-I-Gotta-Know – For-Sure-Baby

(Chorus)
Tell Me The Truth
Do You Love Me Baby
I Know I Should Know It
But I Don't Feel It
Do You Love Me Baby
If You Don't – Let Me Know
So I Can Find Someone That Does

When-We – First-Met – It-Was-All
We-Could-Do – To-Keep-Our
Hands-Off the Other
It-Was so Great – Being in Love
But-Now – I-Know the Truth
You-Don't – Love-Me-Anymore

When-I-Think – About-This-Baby
This-Is-The-Way – It-Should-Be
Because-After-All – My-Wondering
If-You-Love-Me or Not
I-Have-Fallen – Out of Love – With-You

(Chorus)
Tell Me The Truth
Do You Love Me Baby
I Know I Should Know It
But I Don't Feel It
Do You Love Me Baby
If You Don't – Let Me Know
So I Can Find Someone That Does

Deja-Vu (Pages 35-44)

It had been an emotional draining day for everyone, but even more so for Andy and Carrie. Carrie put her hand on Andy's arm to stop him from leaving, "Not even a goodbye kiss Andy?"

Andy shrugged his shoulders slightly and replied, "What's the point Carrie?"

Carrie stared at Andy in disbelief, "What's the point Andy? The point is the past year and a half of our lives together. You are my first love you idiot. I let you and now you do not want to even kiss me goodbye."

Andy sadly replied, "Yes the last year and a half has been great but now it is over."

Carrie wasn't about to give up so easily, "Andy we can write each other maybe on holidays we can even maybe get together."

Andy paced a little then turned back to Carrie and said, "I can not kiss, hug or lay down and love with a letter."

"It's not our fault Andy." A breeze stirred causing Carrie's hair to whip around into her eyes, making them sting even more from unshed tears.

"I know Carrie it's the world's. Our city of hope and dreams is closing down around everyone. You and your family are going north and my family is going south." Andy reached up and brushed the hair from Carrie's eyes.

"Come on Andy, we are young and eighteen, very soon a year will pass the year both of us said we would give to our families. We will be only nineteen when we can finally be together." Carrie put her arms around Andy's waist and looked up into his brown eyes waiting for a response but Andy didn't say anything. "You do love me, don't you Andy?"

Andy finally responded putting his arms around Carrie, "Yes I love you, you are great and easy to love. But..."

"But what Andy?" asked Carrie nervously.

"I have to take care of my family now, Carrie you know this. My dad ran out on us when the plant closed down and he just took off after telling us that we were bad luck and he wanted a new life." Andy could feel the weight pressing down on his young shoulders.

"I know Andy, your dad is a crap head and what he did to you and your family was bad." Carrie tightened her arms around Andy.

"Bad? It is more than bad Carrie he also took off with all the money. We are broke, we are moving in with in-laws that we do not get together with during holidays. My life and college is over with. My mom and I are going to be working at my uncle's store." Andy hugged Carrie a little closer.

"Well at least Andy you have something to fall back on. My family is starting over with no opportunity, just a dream." Carrie laid her head on Andy's chest and sighed.

"That is true but at least all of you are together. Face it Carrie the world sucks, what is the point in pretending?" Andy was getting a little upset with the heavy of it all.

"Because I love you and I don't want to happen what both of us are already thinking in our minds," Carrie was feeling the heaviness of it all in her soul. She wished she didn't feel any doubts in her heart but she couldn't help feeling them.

Andy looked into Carrie's eyes, already knowing her answer but he had to ask,"What is that?"

"Out of sight, out of mind. Like you Andy I too want to be held and loved. I want this to be with you, you know I do but." Carrie stepped back out of Andy's embrace. "But what Carrie?"

"You." Carrie stared at Andy. Andy looked confused, "Me? What about me?"

Carrie shook her head, "Andy you are a man, you have no control. The first pretty thing that smiles at you will get your full attention and I will be forgotten."

"You have a lot of faith in me Carrie. Why do you love me then?"

"Because you have what I like in a man and as long you are near me you have no reason to stray," stated Carrie as it was the truth.

Andy couldn't help himself, he had to grin, "I have what you like? Like what?"

Carrie smiled back, "You are kind, you are loving and you are a great lover."

Andy chuckled, "Yes that is all true especially the great lover part." Both of them laughed at that.

"What are we going to do Andy?" Carrie moved back to Andy for another hug. Andy shrugged his shoulders, "I don't know Carrie."

"I want to be with you Andy forever. I can be myself with you," Carrie could feel tears swimming to the surface again.

"Yes we are broke in and weather proof," Andy smiled at Carrie hoping for another smile from her.

"Broke in? Wow what romantic words come from your mouth. Please no more Andy, I don't think my heart can take it," Carrie put her right hand over her heart.

"Okay I could have put that better." Andy chuckled a little. Carrie grinned and said, "You think?" They both laughed.

"Damn Carrie we are so great together. Yes you are right, I'll probably wait then go for it," Andy said acknowledging Carrie's earlier statement.

"Go for it? You mean cheat don't you?" Carrie began to get upset with Andy all over again.

"How can I cheat on you when you are nowhere to be seen or felt Carrie?" Andy stepped back putting a little space between himself and Carrie.

"What? What kind of answer is that? It does not matter if I'm near you or not, you idiot. I am suppose to be in your heart no matter where you are." Carrie could feel herself getting madder by the second.

"I'm the Idiot and you come out so nice and clean?" Andy stepped away from Carrie and turned to look deeper into the woods.

Carrie walked around to stand in front of Andy again, with hands on her hips she said, "What's that suppose to mean?"

"Are you not the one who said out of sight, out of mind?" asked Andy ready for them to start arguing but hoping they wouldn't.

"Yes, so?" Carrie responded with a shrug of her shoulders.

"Well to me that means you are all ready thinking about getting it on when I'm not around." Andy looked at Carrie waiting for her to deny it.

"Well Andy thinking about it and doing it are two different things. Or don't you know that?" Carrie didn't really want to argue with Andy on their last night together.

"Well how about this? We have about three hours left of our last night together, so I say since we're talking about doing it we just go ahead and do it one more time." Andy reached out and ran his hand gently down Carrie's arm and then took her hand in his.

"I don't know Andy? I don't think my breaking heart could stand that." Carrie squeezed Andy's fingers.

"Yeah right Carrie what about my heart? You cannot say goodbye to me without one more memory." Andy was really hoping to turn this argument around to his favor.

"Okay I guess." Carrie wasn't sure she should but she truly did want to. "So that is yes?" asked Andy hopefully. Carrie smiled and kissed Andy, "Yes that is yes."

Andy smiled glad he was getting his way, "Well don't stand there and waste time woman let's get to striping." Carrie giggled, "After you, man of my dreams." They shared some intimate laughter.

"Andy what am I going to do? I'll never find another man like you." said Carrie, not willing to let it go.

"Yes so true, I am one of a kind. And the same goes for you Carrie, you're hot and cool." Andy doesn't want to ruin his last night with Carrie.

38

"Andy I have an idea." Carrie stood still thinking. "What's that?" asked Andy.

"Let's just get the Hell out of here tonight." Carrie was warming up to this idea quickly.

"That sounds great Carrie. Just jump into a car and drive away from all this heavy. Then later on we can sell it for food and water." Andy was getting tired of all this talk, he was ready for some Loving.

Carrie was not happy with Andy's response so she said tartly, "Well with that attitude forget it."

Andy knew if this night was going to end like he wanted he had to keep Carrie happy. "It's more than that Carrie we will have to borrow one of your dad's cars and your dad will call the cops."

Carrie hugged Andy again, "I know. Just think if it was a year from now we could do whatever we wanted to do because we'd both be free." Andy hugged Carrie closer and said, "Yeah I thought about that, like I said the world sucks so baby let's get it on one more time."

One more time happens and afterwards the two sad young lovers take a walk in the woods to slowly say goodbye to each other. "Hold me Andy."

"My pleasure Carrie. Come here baby." The two sad young lovers hold each other tightly both wishing to themselves this night would never end.

"What was that?" asked Andy staring off into the woods.

"What Andy?" asked Carrie looking from Andy's face to the direction he is staring. "That flash of light over there."

Carrie shakes her head, "I did not see any light Andy."

Andy grabs Carrie's hand and says, "Well I did and I want to go check it out."

"No Andy, it is so dark and I have a bad feeling about this." says Carrie pulling her hand back.

"Stay here then Carrie. Better yet get back in the car and lock the doors. I'll be right back." Andy headed into the woods.

"My butt. No, I go with you I don't want to be alone," said Carrie jogging to catch up to Andy.

Andy takes Carrie's hand again, "Well then come on sexy let's go check out this mysterious light in the dark of night."

Carrie feels shivers run up and down her back. "Knock it off, don't scare me Andy."

"Well if this were a movie Carrie the love scene is over with, now it is time for some fantasy or horror." Andy said enjoying this mystery.

"Stop it Andy, I'm going back to the car." Carrie pulled her hand from Andy's grasp and started back to the car.

"Suit yourself, I got to know," said Andy continuing to walk into the woods. Carrie turned back to Andy, "Damn you Andy, wait up." "Well come on then let's go," said Andy motioning with his hand for Carrie to hurry up.

"Andy why don't you ever listen to me?" asked Carrie out of breath.

"Because I am man. Roar." Andy hit himself in the chest with his fist.

Carrie smirked, "You are idiot you mean. Something is going to happen. I just know it."

Andy grinned and shook his head, "Well think pot of gold and not a sack of crap Carrie."

Carrie brought up their earlier conversation as they trudged through the woods. "Andy are we going to stay together or are we going to let the world keep us apart?"

"I don't know Carrie, I love you, you love me but we are so young, we have our whole lives ahead of us. Do we really want to waste the best years of our lives making the same mistake like so many before us have made?" Andy held a branch out of the way so Carrie could walk through without it hitting her in the face.

Carrie almost stopped in her tracks, "We're a mistake now?"

"No but like you said, out of sight, out of mind. We are young and

I think the both of us should live our lives instead of putting a big heavy on ourselves and each other."

Andy kept walking towards where he saw the flash of light.

Carrie was confused and asked, "What heavy?"

"Being apart and both of us in new places to live. You are going to college Carrie, you should do that. If you get stuck in our funk you'll never go to college. We are too young to make it on our own. College for the both of us would be pure fantasy."

"What is so bad about a fantasy Andy?" demanded Carrie.

"Because for so long I lived with my head in the clouds believing my life was on track and I had nothing to worry about, I was going make it." Andy stopped for a moment and then continued walking.

"And now Andy?" asked Carrie walking faster to keep up with Andy's long strides. Andy thought for a moment, "I feel like Fate has kicked me in my soul letting me know I'm doomed?"

"Andy, Andy, that is why you have me, I'm the one you can count on. Together you and I against the world. Both of us were alone and we found each other. That was Fate Andy, and now Fate is testing us." Carrie felt terrible that all seemed doomed to Andy.

"What are you saying Carrie?" asked Andy stopping to turn and look at Carrie.

"I am telling you, let's live these next two or three months apart with the love of the other in our hearts. You can trust me Andy, I will not screw around. What about you Andy can you say the same to me? And not just words you think I want to hear. No Andy, if you want our lives to be intertwined until we die, you have to feel our love of one another deep inside your heart. It has to be true and strong and without any doubts. I love you Andy and I want to spend the rest of our lives together being in love." Andy hugs Carrie to him tightly, "Carrie I love you, you know I do, I just need time to think."

"Well Andy you have about an hour to think about it before we have to leave and go home, I hope that is enough time because I will want my answer then." Carrie hugged Andy back just as tightly.

41

"Wow a whole hour, no pressure there." Andy turned and started walking again.

"One hour Andy, love me forever or let me go forever." Andy stops and looks at Carrie with I can't believe her and I love her going through his mind.

"How much further is this light you saw Andy? I'm getting cold and tired," complained Carrie.

"I don't know, not too much further I think." Andy and Carrie keep walking further and deeper into the dark, damp woods in silence.

Andy suddenly stops, "I think I see something."

Carrie looks around Andy and asks, "What is it Andy?"

"Let's find out Carrie. Come on whatever it is, it is right there twenty feet in front of us." Andy puts on a little more speed.

"I don't know Andy, I'm scared, aren't you?" states Carrie hanging back. "No." "Why not?"

"Because if there is something in this world or universe as Fate, it is calling to me now and I have to answer it. I am the moth and right over there Carrie is the flame."

Carrie stops walking and says, "Well maybe this is for you and not for me or us. I will stay here Andy, you go grab a hold of your Fate and make it belong to you."

Andy shakes his head, "Damn Carrie that was deep." Carrie pushes Andy and says, "Just move you ass, I'm freezing here."

Andy walks slowly and surely towards something that is shining in the darkness of the woods like a beacon to his eyes. "Carrie it's a car and it's like no car I have seen before." "What do you mean?"

"Well Carrie this car as far as I can tell has never been made. And..." Andy pauses.

"And what Andy? You're scaring me even more now." Carrie rubs her hands up and down her arms trying to warm up.

"Well hold on to yourself tight Carrie because this Fate gets even weirder," says Andy walking up to the car. "How weird?"

"This car has been abandoned for many years." Andy looks in the car window, "Oh God, this cannot be for real."

"What now Andy?"

"There are two people in this car and they have been dead for a while now." Andy reaches for the car door handle.

"Gross. Andy get away from there. Let's go back to the car and we can drive to the police station. Better yet let's just give them a call. Here I'll give them a call right now. They can fool with the dead bodies and I can go home to my bed and hide under the covers." Carrie snaps her cell phone closed, "Damn no signal. Let's go back to the car and call the police, please Andy."

"Hang on a second, I almost have the driver's door open, it's stuck really good." Andy tugs harder on the door.

"Stop Andy, don't open that door. Think about it. How could you have seen a light from a car that has been out here for who knows how long with dead bodies in it?" Carrie is really freaking out.

"What?" "Think about it, you know I am right. Let's get the Hell out of here." Carrie starts hopping from one foot to another. "I got it Carrie, it's opening up. I cannot believe this!"

"Believe what Andy?" Andy does not answer Carrie he just stands there frozen looking into the car with disbelief. "Andy tell me already. What is wrong with you? Say something to me." Andy tries his best but the words he wants to say will not come forth from out of his mouth.

Carrie cannot take the suspense any longer and slowly walks over to the mystery car so she can see for herself what has freaked her lover out so much. When she arrives, Carrie stops right beside Andy, looks at him standing there unable to talk and frozen solid with fear. Carrie cannot believe how Andy is and then takes her eyes off of Andy and looks in the open driver's door into the car.

"What? Oh my God! This cannot be for real! Please take this sight from my eyes, I cannot look at it anymore!"

"Carrie, what you see is for real. In this car, that has not been made yet, sits the two of us years from now and both of us are dead."

Carrie grabs Andy by his arm and pulls at it for him to come with her and as far away from this crazy car as they can get from it. Andy blinks his eyes, then turns towards Carrie and says to her with undying love for her in his voice. "Carrie we were together when we died, many, many years from now. Fate has spoken to us, letting us know for sure that we are meant to be together forever."

"Okay, okay, Fate has spoken to us Andy, now let's get the Hell out of here." Carrie pulls harder on Andy's arm and he finally moves.

Andy and Carrie quickly walk to the spot where Andy first saw the car shining in the darkness. They are about to keep on walking when from behind them the abandoned car starts up its engine like it is brand new. Andy and Carrie stop walking and turn around to look at something else that is impossible. There for both of their eyes to see are the older versions of themselves standing outside of the car smiling at them. They wave goodbye and then both of them step back into the running car and then they and the car disappear right in front of Andy's and Carrie's eyes.

"What is going on Andy?" a pleading Carrie asks.

"I don't know and I do not care Carrie. The only thing I care about is your answer to my question." Andy pulls Carrie to him.

"What question Andy?" asks Carrie scared but full of curiosity

"Will you marry me Carrie?" asks Andy kissing Carrie softly on the lips. "What?" Carrie cannot believe what she is hearing.

"Will you marry me Carrie? I love you with all my heart and I want to spend the rest of my life with you." Andy waits expectantly.

Carrie looks at Andy with disbelieving eyes, then tears come to those same eyes as she gets Fate's plan for them and says to a waiting Andy, "Yes Andy I will marry you. I love you with all my heart."

Book Ten: Thunder Love (Pages 45-78)
(The Numbers after the Song Titles are the Original Numbering. Every Song in this Book is a **New Song** Written for this Book, minus the B's)

(Side One)
181. Thunder Love (605.)
     I'm The Thunder Love **(935.)**
182. Sun Baked Lover (638.)
     Give Me Sun **(929.)**
183. Heart-Breaker (637.)
     Love Breaker **(936.)**
184. Who's Next (639.)
185. Tidal Wave Of Sex (640.)

(Side Two)
(Yesterday – Today and Some Days After That 186-187)
186. Without Saying Good-Bye (649.)
187. **PT-1:** I Like You Now / **PT-2:** I Don't Like You Now (650.)
188. 15 Minutes (652.)
     15 Minutes Ago / 5 More Minutes Please **(937.)**
189. It's Your Fault (And You Know It) (653.)
190. Why Say No – When You Can Say Yes (654.)

(Side Three)
191. Do You Like To Rock (655.)
     Come Over And Rock Me **(938.)**
192. Love Zone (656.)
193. Say Lust – Not Love (657.)
194. The Dark Side Of Love (658.)
195. Get Hot For Me (659.)
     Get High For Me **(939.)**

(Side Four)
196. The Both Of You (660.)
197. It's Time To Do It (661.)
     It's Time To Rock **(940.)**
198. Making Love (AKA: Bath Time Sex) (662.)
199. Rock And Roll Lovers (664.)
200. Kiss Of Death (665.)

(Bonus Songs)
Lady From Space (Sex Version) (347.) / I Had A Lot Better (404.)

181. Thunder Love

Thunder-Loving – Super-Ready
I-Take-This-Hot – Loving-Night
With-My-Giant – Thunder-Love
Searching-For the Right-Ones
That-Loves – Some-Fine-Loving

I'm-The-One – Yes-I-Am
That-Can – Take-You-Higher
To the Height of Your-Desire
If-You-Want – This-Lovin' of Mine
All-You-Gotta-Do – Is-Join-In

(Chorus)
Thunder Love / Across The Sky
Great Looking Bodies On Fire
That Lustfully Burn With Desire
When They're In Thunder Loving Motion
So Come On Baby – Let's Thunder Love
Let's Thunder Love – Until You Pass Out

Where-You-Going – Pretty
Fine – Thunder-Loving-Lady
I'm-Only – Half-Way-Through
Don't-Leave – These-Three
Ladies-All-Alone – Trying to Cope
With-My – Thunder-Love

That's-OK – Take-Your-Moment
I-Understand – Completely-Baby
Believe-Me – I-Know-That-My
Thunder-Love is Intense – And the Reason
You-Never – Want to Leave

(Chorus)
Thunder Love / Across The Sky
Great Looking Bodies On Fire
That Lustfully Burn With Desire
When They're In Thunder Loving Motion
So Come On Baby – Let's Thunder Love
Let's Thunder Love – Until You Pass Out

46

I'm The Thunder Love

Say-Goodbye to Sadness
Say-Goodbye to Loneliness
Say-Goodbye to Hate
Say-Goodbye to War
Because – I'm-Coming

Love's-Time is Here
I'm-Here to Break-Down
All the Walls – That-Surround-Us
If-This-Ain't – Quite-Clear
I'm-Saying – Forget-Fear
And-Bring-Forth – Your-Love

(Chorus)
Holy Love – Holy Sex
I'm The Thunder Love
Ain't No Plundering
When I'm Around
Just Lots Of Love
For I'm The Thunder Love
And I'm Coming To Spread My Love

Love-Times is Here
I'm-Here to Break-Down
All the Walls – That-Surround-Us
If-This-Ain't – Quite-Clear
I'm-Saying – Forget-Fear
And-Bring-Forth – Your-Love

(Chorus)
Holy Love – Holy Sex
I'm The Thunder Love
Ain't No Plundering
When I'm Around
Just Lots Of Love
For I'm The Thunder Love
And I'm Coming To Spread My Love

182. Sun Baked Lover

Taking a Walk – In the Park
Letting the Hot-Sun
Shine-Down on My
Searching – For-Lust-Body

Looking at All the Lovers
Makes-Me-Frown
Where-Are – All the Single
Hot – Lonely – Lovers
That-Only-Want – To-Get-Naked
And-Have-Sex – Out-In-The-Sun

(Chorus)
Sun Baked Lover
You Are So Fine
I Want To Sex-Bake
Out In The Sun With You
Until My Butt Gets Sunburned

Come-On-Baby – Sunburn-Your-Butt – With-Me
Come-On-Baby – Sunburn-Your-Butt – With-Me
Then-Let's-Go and Sit-In-Some – Cool-Water

We-See – We-Lick-Our-Lips
I-Point to The-Little – Woods in The-Park
She-Nods – Her-Head-Yes

We're-Loving – So-Hard
As-We – Turn and Turn
While – Burning and Burning
Lusting-This-Moment – Like-It's a Gift

(Chorus)
Sun Baked Lover
You Are So Fine
I Want To Sex-Bake
Out In The Sun With You
Until My Butt Gets Sunburned

Come-On-Baby – Sunburn-Your-Butt – With-Me
Come-On-Baby – Sunburn-Your-Butt – With-Me
Then-Let's-Go and Sit-In-Some – Cool-Water

48

Give Me Sun

Sun – Sun – Sun / Give – Me – Sun
Sun – Sun – Sun / Give – Me – Sun

Remember-Everybody – Having-Sun
Is-Better-Than – No-Sun at All
Now-Let's – Start-This – Sun-Song

I-Pick-Up – My-Happy-Soul
Zipping-My-Pants – While
Putting a Smile – On-My-Face

My-Moment is Over – Time to Realize
I've-Sexed it Up – 'Til-Dawn
Saying the Old-Saying
Today is Another-Day
To-Repeat – My-No-Mistakes

(Chorus)
It's A Beautiful Day / With No Need to Pray
Give – Me – Sun / Give – Me – Sun
For The Sun Is Shining – Down Into My Soul
Give – Me – Sun / Give – Me – Sun
It's A Beautiful Day / With No Need to Pray
Give – Me – Sun / Give – Me – Sun
For The Sun Is Shining – Down Into My Soul
Give – Me – Sun / Give – Me – Sun

I-Love the Sun – Sadly it Has-Set
Bring-On – The-Night
Where-Love is Replaced – With-Lust

Mary – Sally or Betty – Maybe-All-Three
Choices-Choices – With-Many-Hours – 'Til-Dawn
Pedal to The-Metal – Big-City – Here-I-Come

(Chorus)
It's A Beautiful Day / With No Need to Pray
Give – Me – Sun / Give – Me – Sun
For The Sun Is Shining – Down Into My Soul
Give – Me – Sun / Give – Me – Sun
(Repeat)

183. Heart-Breaker

She-Came – Into-My – Slow-Life
Like a Full-Running – Sexy-Love-Train
Full of Sweet – Hot
You-Can-Have-Me – Because
I-Want-You – To-Have-Me-Ability

Enjoyed-I-Did – She-Was-Great
I-Went – Sex-Blind
Trying-To – Out-Do-Myself
Every-Time – She-Allowed-Me
To-Take-Off – My-Clothes

(Chorus)
Heart-Breaker – Heart-Breaker
Ripping Out My Helpless-Heart
Heart-Breaker – Heart-Breaker
Her Love-Claws – Slice So Deep
Heart-Breaker – Heart-Breaker
Has Left Me Heart-Broken
Over-Sexed-Crazy And Without
Any Of My Damn Money

Love is Blind – Sex-Makes-You – Dumb
I-Didn't-Care – About-Anything-Else
I-Dropped-My-Life – To the Side
As-I-Waited – Every-Night
For-My-Future – Heart-Breaker
To-Lead-Me-To – The-Ecstasy of Sex-Love

The-Power to Take – Every-Thing
I-Own – In-This
Whole – Wide – World
Lies-Between – Her-Thighs
I-Only-Wish – I-Had-More to Give-Her
So-She-Could – Sex-Take-It – Away-From-Me- Again

(Chorus)
Heart-Breaker – Heart-Breaker / Ripping Out My Helpless-Heart
Heart-Breaker – Heart-Breaker / Her Love-Claws – Slice So Deep
Heart-Breaker – Heart-Breaker / Has Left Me Heart-Broken
Over-Sexed-Crazy And Without / Any Of My Damn Money

Love Breaker

She-Loves-You
Your-Heart-Belongs to Her
Everything is Great
You're at Peace
Expecting-Nothing – Besides-Love

Out of The-Corner of Your-Eye
You-See-Her – Smiling at You
Not-Realizing – That-Any-Moment
She's-Going to Strike – At-Your-Heart
Ready or Not – Here-She-Comes

(Chorus)
Your Lover Has Gone Sour
And You Don't Even Know It
Your Lover Is A Very Cold
Love Breaker
That Eats Up Your Love
Until You Have None Left

You-Scream – You-Try to Run-Away
With-Only a Morsel of Love
Left-Inside – Your-Heart
No-Good – You're too Slow
And-She is Still-Hungry
For the Rest of Your-Love

Why-Me – You-Scream
The-Answers is Quite-Clear
You're a Fool in Love
Ready or Not – Here-She-Comes
Chomping-Her-Teeth – To-Eat
The-Last-Bit – Of-Your-Love – Out of Your-Heart

(Chorus)
Your Lover Has Gone Sour
And You Don't Even Know It
Your Lover Is A Very Cold
Love Breaker
That Eats Up Your Love
Until You Have None Left

51

184. Who's Next

Sex-Party-Night – Fifty-Couples-Strong
Freedom-Reigns – When-Lust
Flows-Free – With-Many
Different-Partners – In-One-Night

There is No-Shame – For-Any of Us
We-Are-Not – Doing-Anything-Wrong
It's-Our-Bodies – It's-Our-Life
We-Have The Right – To-Sex-Swing

(Chorus)
Who's Next
I've Just Enjoyed Myself
And I'd Like To Do It Again
So – Who's Next
I'm Ready For Some More
Of Whatever You Got
So Come On Baby – Be My Next
Sex Moment Of The Night

Be-Almost-Polite – While-You're
Enjoying-Yourself – With-Another
That-Is-Not – Your-Lover
By-Remembering – That-They're
Someone's-Lover as Well

Enjoy-Yourself – Very-Much
Help-Them – Do the Same
It-Might-Be – Their-First-Time
They're-Nervous – They're-Turned-On
It's-Up to You to Show-Them
What-Free-Swinging-Sex – Is-All-About

(Chorus)
Who's Next
I've Just Enjoyed Myself
And I'd Like To Do It Again
So – Who's Next
I'm Ready For Some More
Of Whatever You Got
So Come On Baby – Be My Next
Sex Moment Of The Night
52

185. Tidal Wave Of Sex

What-Am-I – Thinking-With
Is-Not – That-Hard to Understand
Been-Wanting to Do-This
For so Long – My-Whole-Life

This is My-Night to Soar
This is My-Night to Score
With-Two-Ladies – In-One-Night
That-Don't-Know the Other
Or – About-My-Greedy – Sex-Plan
That-Involves-One – Then the Other

(Chorus)
If I Can Time This Just Right
I Can Bring Myself A Giant
Tidal Wave Of Sex
All Over My Lust Full Body
That Wants To Enjoy
The Height Of Passion   Twice
Because I'm So Very Nice

It-Was-Hard – But-I-Succeeded
It-Took – Some-Smooth-Talking
For-Me to Get-My – First-Date
To-Want-Her – Dessert-First

Kinda-Tired but Pumped and Ready
I-Took-My-Time – With-My-Second-Date
Then-Like – The-Sex-King of The-World
I-Had a Reason – To-Smile – Twice as Big
And-Say – I-Did-It – I-Finally-Did-It

(Chorus)
If I Can Time This Just Right
I Can Bring Myself A Giant
Tidal Wave Of Sex
All Over My Lust Full Body
That Wants To Enjoy
The Height Of Passion – Twice
Because I'm So Very Nice

53

186. Without Saying Good-Bye

We-Met – We-Got it On
I-Left – In the Early – Morning-Light
Not-Looking-Back for More
Of-What – You-Just-Gave-Me

You-Got-Mad – You-Called-Me-Names
I-Didn't – Take it Personal
You-Were – Just-Releasing – Your-Blues
Of-Letting-Me – Touch-You – With-Both-Hands
Before-I-Even-Knew – Your-Favorite-Color

(Chorus)
I Thought About It Baby
Lovers Come And Lovers Go
You Were A Great Lover – Baby
That I Should Have Sampled Twice
So What I'm Saying To You – Baby
Is That I'd Like To Start Over – Like I Never
Left You After – Without Saying Good-Bye First

Week-Later – I-Show-Up – At-Your-Door
Knocking-Like – I-Want-Some-Lovin'
I'm-Looking so Fine – You-Have to Say-Yes
I-Wait and I-Wait – Finally – There-You-Are
Looking-Like – You've-Been-Waiting on Me

I-Never-Apologize – I-Snap-My-Fingers
Watching-You – Move to The-Side – So-I-Can
Squeeze-Myself – Slowly – Through the Opening
That-You-Are – Allowing-Me to Have

Got to Play – This-Cool
You're so Hot – Looking
Don't-Wanna – Take the Chance
You-Won't-Say – Yes to Twice

(Chorus)
I Thought About It Baby
Lovers Come And Lovers Go
You Were A Great Lover – Baby
That I Should Have Sampled Twice
So What I'm Saying To You – Baby
Is That I'd Like To Start Over – Like I Never
Left You After – Without Saying Good-Bye First

I-Lick-Your-Neck – As-You-Slowly
Close the Door – I-Kiss-Your-Lips
As-You – Begin to Shake and Moan
I'm-All – You-Remembered
Even-Though – You-Hate-Me
You're-Glad – You're-Letting-Me
Sample-Your-Goods – One-More-Time

That's it Baby – Lose-Control
While-I'm-Holding-You – As-You
Melt and Purr in My-Arms – As-I
Slowly-Lead-Us – To-Your-Bedroom

(Chorus)
I Thought About It Baby
Lovers Come And Lovers Go
You Were A Great Lover – Baby
That I Should Have Sampled Twice
So What I'm Saying To You – Baby
Is That I'd Like To Start Over – Like I Never
Left You After – Without Saying Good-Bye First

The-Promise-Land – Is at Hand – When-You
Like a Sexy-Vixen – Snap-Your-Fingers
Right into My-Starring – Lustful-Eyes

You're in Total-Control – When-There's-No
On-Your-Lips – As-I-Begin to Beg
On-My-Knees – As-You – Bring-Me-My-Collar

Leash-In-Your-Hand – I-Follow-You to Where
You're-Going to Tie-Me-Up – So-I-Stay-This-Time

(Repeat Chorus)

187. PT-1: I Like You Now

I'm-Your-Man-Pet
You-Keep-Me – With-Food and Water
With-Only-Enough – Love-Sex
To-Keep-You – Satisfied

I-Bring-You – Your-Shoes
You-Make-Me – Put-Them-On-You
I-Bring-You – My-Body
When-You're-Nice – We-Play
When-I'm-Bad – I'm-Punished
Put in My-Spot – Where-I-Spend
The-Night – On the Floor – All-Alone

(Chorus)
You Take Away My Blanket
You Pull My Pillow From
Underneath Me – When I'm Sleeping
You Make Me Beg For Sex
Miss-Love – I Like You Now
Can You Tell Me – I'm A Bad Man Again

You-Come-Home – It's-My-Fault
You've-Had a Bad-Day – Today
You-Grab-Me – By-My-Hair
Telling-Me – You-Don't-Want
Anything to Do – With-Me-Tonight

In-My-Spot – You're-Getting-Ready
Things-Have-Changed – First-Time
My-Key to My-Lock – In-Your-Purse
As-You-Leave-Me – To-Go-Out – On a Date

(Chorus)
You Take Away My Blanket
You Pull My Pillow From
Underneath Me – When I'm Sleeping
You Make Me Beg For Sex
Miss-Love – I Like You Now
Can You Tell Me – I'm A Bad Man Again

187. Pt-2: I Don't Like You Now

I-Use to Like – Your-Face
I-Use to Like – Your-Body
Now-I-Think – They-Both-Suck
As-Much – As-Your-Heart-Does

I-Used-You-Once – Making-You-Cry
I-Came-Back – One-More-Time
Damn – Did-I-Pay the Price – You've-Snapped
Gone-From-Lovely – Hot-Mistress
To-Thinking – That-You-Really – Own-Me

(Chorus)
I Don't Like You Now
You're No More Fun
The Sex You Brought
Was Something I Lived For
I Don't Like You Now
You're No More Fun – Because
The Sex You Bring Now
Belongs To Someone Else First

You-Come-Home – All-Drunk
Forgetting-About – Your-Man-Pet
Take-My-Key – From-Your-Purse
While-You-Fall-Asleep – On the Couch

What a Bitch – You-Turned-Out to Be
I-Can't-Believe – I-Use to Like-You
At-Least – I've-Learned the Hard-Way
Which-Head to Think-With
When it Comes – To a Lady-Like-You

(Chorus)
I Don't Like You Now
You're No More Fun
The Sex You Brought
Was Something I Lived For
I Don't Like You Now
You're No More Fun – Because
The Sex You Bring Now
Belongs To Someone Else

188. 15 Minutes

Love Me – Love-You / It's the Same-Thing
I-Got-What-You-Want / You-Got-What-I-Need
We-Get-It-On / Then-We're-Gone
Like-We – Don't-Know the Other

Few-Moments-Later – Wanting-More-Of
What-Made-Us – Feel so Alive
You-Look at Me – With-Gleaming-Eyes
I-Come-Up to You and Say

(Chorus)
Just Give Me 15 Minutes
Pretty – Lover – Lady
That's All I Need
Just Give Me 15 Minutes
Then I'll Be Ready
For Some More Of You
Just Give Me 15 Minutes
I'll Make You Moan And Purr
Just Like You Did A Moment Ago

We-Were-Wild / We-Were-Free
We're-Spent / We-Want-More
You-Look at Me – Saying
You – Have – Needs

It's-Been too Long
Since-You – Felt-This-Way
It's-Up to Me – To-Make-This-Happen
Over and Over – 'Til-You're-Done – With-Me
I-Look-Over – At-You and Say

(Chorus)
Just Give Me 15 Minutes
Pretty – Lover – Lady
That's All I Need
Just Give Me 15 Minutes
Then I'll Be Ready
For Some More Of You
Just Give Me 15 Minutes
I'll Make You Moan And Purr
Just Like You Did A Moment Ago
58

15 Minutes Ago / 5 More Minutes Please

I-Touch-Your-Face
It's as Pretty as Your-Soul
You're-Always-Glowing
Ready for More-Loving
While-I'm-Trying to Keep-Up

Baby-I'm-Trying
I-Want to Be – The-Man
That's-Always-Ready
To-Make-You – Scream-Out-Loud
But-Sorry-Baby – I'm-Getting too Old

(Chorus #1)
15 Minutes Ago – I Was Doing Great
15 Minutes Ago – I Was Making Love
For The Third Time This Night
15 Minutes Ago – My Heart Stopped Beating
Now I'm a Soul – With No One To Screw
(Repeat Chorus #1)

Hello-Death – I-Know-Why – You're-Here
It's-Time for You to Take-Me to Heaven
I'm-Ready and All – Death – But
Can-You – Do-Me a Favor-First
Here-Check-This-Out

(Chorus #2)
Death – I Know I'm Dead
But I'm Not Quite Ready
To Go To Heaven Yet
I Was In The Middle Of
Making Love – When I Died
So Death – Be A Sport And Give Me
5 More Minutes Please
Then I'll Be Glad To Go To Heaven
(Repeat Chorus #2)

What-Was-That-Death
What-Do-You-Mean
I'm-Not Going To Heaven
Where am I Going-Then
Oh-No – You-Can't be Serious
59

189. It's Your Fault (And You Know It)

Time-After-Time – You-Cheat
On-Me – Like-I-Don't
Give-You – Want-You-Want
It's so Sad – That-You

Make-Me – Do the Same
Getting-It-On – With the Hottest
Ladies-That-Know – How to Shake
Their-Tails to Please a Fast
Looking for Sex – Kinda-Man

(Chorus)
Baby – It's Your Fault
And You Know It
You Cheat So Much
It's All I Can Do
To Keep Up With Your
Cheating Ways – Baby

You-Tell-Me – You-Have a
Free-Living – Life-Style
That-One-Man – Can't-Hang
With-Your-Hot – Sexual-Ways
I-Tell-You to Stick-Around
For 15 Minutes

I-Will – Rock-You
Like-You – Need to Be-Rocked
'Cause-Baby – I've-Got a Blessing
Between – My – Legs
That-Out-Shines – The-Mightiest
Like a Tree – To a Stick

(Chorus)
Baby – It's Your Fault
And You Know It
You Cheat So Much
It's All I Can Do
To Keep Up With Your
Cheating Ways – Baby

190. Why Say No – When You Can Say Yes

I-Unzip – My-Attitude
You-Shake – Your-Head-No
I-Put-My-Pants – On the Floor
You-Nod – Your-Head-Yes
With a Flushing-Face – And a Ready to Go-Body

I'm a Man – That-Knows
How to Make a Woman
Regret – Her – Decision
With a Smile – On-Her-Lips
So-Baby – How-About-This

(Chorus)
Why Say No
When You Can Say Yes
Don't Hesitate Baby
Let's Rock And Roll
Before I Have To Roll Away And
Give My Attitude To Someone Else

We-Smiled-Once – We-Smile-Twice
The-Look in Your-Eyes – While
Holding-Your-Breath – Impatiently
For-My 15 Minutes to Be-Over-With
Makes-Your-Mind – Start to Rewind
What-You-Did – Lovingly-Twice

Ashamed for Being so Weak
Thinking too Much-About
Having-Sex – With a Man
You-Just-Met a Few-Hours-Ago
I-Recognize – Your-Look and Say
Baby – How-About-This

(Chorus)
Why Say No
When You Can Say Yes
Don't Hesitate Baby
Let's Rock And Roll
Before I Have To Roll Away And
Give My Attitude To Someone Else

191. Do You Like To Rock

I-See-You – Once
I-See-You – Twice
You-Shake – Your-Body
Like-You – Want-Me to Want-It
So-Very – Sexy-Bad

I-Try to Catch-Up to You
Your-Shake – Is so Fast
It-Slows – Me-Down
Watching – What-I-Want – As-I
Watch-Your-Fine – Behind
Getting-Further – Away-From-Me

(Chorus)
I Catch My Breath
Say To You – Baby
Do You Like To Rock
'Cause I'd Like To Rock You
With My Rock Hard –Thunder-Love
If You Got The Time To Slow Your Shake

You-Stop – Your-Shaking
Turning-Around to Check-Out
The-Man – Who-Thinks
He-Has-It in Him to Make-You
Slow – Down – Enough
Making-Your-Shaking – Turn to Lust

In-Your-Eyes – I-Can-Tell
That-I-Have to Be – As-Quick-As
Your-Very-Fine – Shake
To-Allow-Me – My-Chance-To
Rock and Roll – You

(Chorus)
I Catch My Breath
Say To You – Baby
Do You Like To Rock
'Cause I'd Like To Rock You
With My Rock Hard –Thunder-Love
If You Got The Time To Slow Your Shake

Come Over And Rock Me

Baby – Let-Me-Tell-You
I-Don't-Want – Dinner
I-Don't-Want – Wine
I-Don't-Want to See a Movie

Baby – Let-Me-Tell-You
I-Don't-Want to Go-Dancing
I-Don't-Want to See-Your-Friends
Baby – I-Just-Want-You-To

(Chorus)
Come Over And Rock Me
'Cause I'm Hot And Horny
Come Over And Rock Me Baby
'Cause I Have Nothing Else To Do
Come Over And Rock Me Baby
Mr. Happy Still Loves You
So Come On Baby
Come Over And Rock Me   Then Get Gone

Baby – Let-Me-Tell-You
I-Don't-Want – Dinner
I-Don't-Want – Wine
I-Don't-Want to See a Movie

Baby-Let-Me-Tell-You
I-Don't-Want to Go-Dancing
I-Don't-Want to See-Your-Friends
Baby – I-Just-Want-You-To

(Chorus)
Come Over And Rock Me
'Cause I'm Hot And Horny
Come Over And Rock Me Baby
'Cause I Have Nothing Else To Do
Come Over And Rock Me Baby
Mr. Happy Still Loves You
So Come On Baby
Come Over And Rock Me – Then Get Gone

192. The Love Zone

Feel – My – Heartbeat
Look-Into-My-Eyes
I-Lust-You-Baby
Let's-Get it On

I'm-More-Than-Ready
To-Start-Up-My – Love-Engine
For-Your-Loving – Pleasures
That-Will-Last – All-Night-Long

(Chorus)
Baby It's Time To Enter
The Love Zone
Don't Worry About Self Control
Leave Ever Thing To Me
Because Baby When I'm In
The Love Zone
I Don't Stop 'Til Dawn

Good-Morning – You're-Welcome
I-Feel-Great – Today
You're-Just – What-I-Wanted
I'm-Glad-I-Have – What-You-Needed

Now-That-Our – Love-Zone is Over
Baby it's Time – For-Me to Say – Goodbye
Don't-Cry / Don't-Get-Mad
I-Don't-Mind – Coming-Back-Tonight
It-Gives-Me-Pleasure – Helping-Out a Fine
Lady-Like-You – Out of Your – Love-Rut

(Chorus)
Baby It's Time To Enter
The Love Zone
Don't Worry About Self Control
Leave Ever Thing To Me
Because Baby When I'm In
The Love Zone
I Don't Stop 'Til Dawn

(This page is blank, for it's the very first, your chance to Mind Rock page. Below are some words for you to use, use one, use them all or use none of them, for this is your very own Mind Rockin' Page, do as you wish, have a Laugh, have a release or both.)

1. Love 2. Sad 3. Happy 4. Sexy 5.Sorrow 6. Life 7. Death 8. I 9. We 10. Remember 11. Forgotten 12. Sky 13. Water 14. Hot 15. Cold 16. Great 17. Bad 18. Earth 19. Heaven 20. Hell

193. Say Lust – Not Love

You-Tell-Me – That-You-Love-Me
I-Tell-You – Goodbye
You-Beg – For-Me to Stay
Telling-Me – That-I'm-Breaking
Your – Lonely – Heart

I-Tell-You – It's-Your – Own-Fault
Baby-You-Know – Quite-Well
I'm a Luster – Not a Lover
With a Message – For-You

(Chorus)
Say Lust – Not Love
To Me Darling
That Way Darling
You Don't Have To Worry
About Me Breaking Your Heart
So Pretty Lonely Darling
Say Lust – Not Love – To Me
Then Maybe I'll Stick Around

It's-Been – 33-Times of Lust
I-Keep-You on a Short-Leash
You-Hate and Love-Me so Much
I-Use-This to Keep – Lusting-You-More

Then-One-Time – Out of Weakness
I-Tell-You – That-I – Love-You
With-New – Power-Inside-You
You-Push-Me-Away – Shaking-Your-Head
With a Message for Me

(Chorus)
Say Lust – Not Love
To Me Darling
That Way Darling
You Don't Have To Worry
About Me Breaking Your Heart
So Handsome Lonely Darling
Say Lust – Not Love – To Me
Then Maybe I'll Stick Around

66

194. The Dark Side Of Love

She-Fell in Love – Very-Young
He-Loved-Her – For a Month
Then-One-Day – He-Was-Gone
Without a So-Long or Goodbye

Days-Later – She-Sees-Him
In the Arms of Another – Lover
Giving-Her the Same-Kind of Love
That-She-Loved
And-Misses so Much

(Chorus)
Welcome Heart Broken
To The Dark Side Of Love
Where There Are No Rules
Just Wanted Moments
That Can Be Shared By Someone
That Wants To Use You
And Not Love You In Return

She's a Lover – That is Not-Loved
She-Feels-This – Inside-Her-Heart
It-Brings-Her – Down to Sadness
That-He – Does-Not – Love-Her

With-No-Reason to Stay
She-Tells-Her – Non-Lover-Goodbye
He-Promises to Change
To-Show-Her – More-Love – Which is
Nothing-But-Lies to Get-Her to Stay
So-She-Leaves – Before-Her
Love-Can-Become – Jaded

(Chorus)
Welcome Heart Broken
To The Dark Side Of Love
Where There Are No Rules
Just Wanted Moments
That Can Be Shared By Someone
That Wants To Use You
And Not Love You In Return

195. Get Hot For Me

I'm-Down – In the Love-Dumps
You-Come-Around – For-Some-Fun
Bringing-Me-Down – Even-More
'Cause-You're so Nice and Sweet

You-Take-Your – Claws
Using-Them as You
Dig-Out – My-Heart
I-Tell-You to Fly-Away
You-Stick-Around – All-High
Watching-Me – Suffer in Delight
As-You-Kick-Around – My-Feelings

(Chorus)
Stop Your Teasing – Baby
I Need Some Action
I'm All Cocked And Loaded
And You're So Damn Fine
So Why Don't You – Get Hot For Me
Instead Of Busting My Balls

I-Go-For-It – With-Your-Claws
Freshly-Sharpened – To-Daggers
You-Slash – Making-Me-Bleed
You-Take a Pause to Taste
What-You-Love – Making-Me-Spill

You're-My-Manhood's – Best-Friend
But-You're a Pain – In-My-Soul
Take-It and I-Take-It – Hoping
One-Day-Soon – You'll-Lose – Your-Appeal
Then-I-Can-Finally – Pull-Your-Claws – Out of My-Flesh

(Chorus)
Stop Your Teasing – Baby
I Need Some Action
I'm All Cocked And Loaded
And You're So Damn Fine
So Why Don't You
Get Hot For Me
Instead Of Busting My Balls

Get High For Me

I-Don't-Need a Beer
I-Don't-Need a Shot of Whiskey
I-Don't-Need a Pill
I-Don't-Need to Do a Line
To-Get – High-For-You
Why – Do – You
When it Comes to Loving-Me
Baby – Is-This-Your-Love
Or-Do-You – Just-Like to Get-High

(Chorus)
Baby – Get High For Me
My Love Is Better Than
Alcohol And Drugs
Baby – Get High For Me
My Love – Will Get You Higher
Than Alcohol And Drugs

Baby – I-Don't-Want to Be a Drag
But-Baby – Once-In a While
I-Need-You to Get-High for Me
Instead of Getting-High – Just to Get-High
Baby – I-Don't-Want to Be a Bummer
Baby – Once-In a While
I-Need-You to Get-High on Our-Love
Instead of Getting-High – Just to Get-High

(Chorus)
Baby – Get High For Me
My Love Is Better Than
Alcohol And Drugs
Baby – Get High For Me
My Love – Will Get You Higher
Than Alcohol And Drugs

Baby – Our-Love
Has-Become a Bad-Trip
I-Want-You – High on Love
I-Want-You – High on Life
Not-High – Out of Your-Mind
All – The-Loving – Time
(Repeat Chorus)

196. The Both Of You

You-Call – Each-Other-Names
You-Fight – Like-Two – Sex-Cats
All the Time – Never-Blaming-Me
It's-Not-My-Fault – Because
I'm-Only a Horny-Man

You-Two – Look so Fine – All-Dirty
With-Your – Clothes-Hanging-Off
With-Hair – Between-Your-Claws
All-Because – You-Want to Be
My-One and Only-Lover

(Chorus)
Well – All I Can Say To You
My Two Lovers Is
I Can't Choose – I Like
The Both Of You
Because – Together As One
You Become – The Perfect Lover

Life is So-Wonderful
I-Kiss-One – I-Kiss the Other
My-Lovers – Love and Hate-This
But-I-Leave – Them-No-Choice
Because – They-Both-Know

I'm-All-That – And-More
That's-Why – I-Can – More-Than-Hang
With-Both of Them – Every-Night
As-They-Bicker-About – Who-Goes-First
And-Who – Gets to Go – Next-Time

(Chorus)
Well – All I Can Say To You
My Two Lovers Is
I Can't Choose – I Like
The Both Of You
Because – Together As One
You Become – The Perfect Lover

197. It's Time To Do It

She-Looks-Sweet – She-Looks-Neat
I-Liked to Quick-Love-Her
Then-Maybe – Ask-Her – Her-Name

I'm a Great – Loving-Man
That-Likes-My – Sexy-Thrills
I'll-Drop-My-Pants – At the Beat of a Heart
Never-Once-Worrying – If-I'm-Making
A-Sexual-Loving – Mistake

(Chorus)
Come On Sweet Love
It's Time To Do It
Right Here Right Now
Let Me Turn You Into A
Sweet Lover – That Is Willing
If You Want This – Sweet Love
All We Got To Do – Is Do It
And Do It – Lots And Lots More

My-Proposal – Turns into Madness
As this Sweet-Love – Lady
Walks-Away – Cursing-Me
For-Thinking – I'm-All-That

With-No-Fear – In-My-Heart
Because-This – Has-Happened-Before
I-Know – Just-What to Do – About-It
Take-Off – My-Clothes – And
Show-Her-My – Do-It and Do-It-Body

(Chorus)
Come On Sweet Love
It's Time To Do It
Right Here Right Now
Let Me Turn You Into A
Sweet Lover – That Is Willing
If You Want This – Sweet Love
All We Got To Do – Is Do It
And Do It – Lots And Lots More

It's Time To Rock

We've-Been – Nice and Slow
We've-Been – Hot and Ready
But-Baby – I-Want-More
Like-You in My-Bed – All-Night

Baby – I'll-Cook-Us-Dinner
Baby – I'll-Buy-The-Wine
Baby – I'll-Even – Wash-My-Sheets
Baby – All-You-Have to Do-Is
Supply the Dessert
I'll-Take-Care of Everything-Else

(Chorus)
Baby You're Fine – Baby I'm A Stud
Sweet Baby It's Time – It's Time To Rock
We've Waited Long Enough
It's Time To Rock
Baby You Know You Want Me
So Come Over And Rock With Me
Because Sweet Baby – It's Time To Rock

We've-Been – Nice and Slow
We've-Been – Hot and Ready
But-Baby – I-Want-More
Like-You in My-Bed – All-Night

Baby – I'll-Cook-Us-Dinner
Baby – I'll-Buy-The-Wine
Baby – I'll-Even – Wash-My-Sheets
Baby – All-You-Have to Do-Is
Supply the Dessert
I'll-Take-Care of Everything-Else

(Chorus)
Baby You're Fine – Baby I'm A Stud
Sweet Baby It's Time – It's Time To Rock
We've Waited Long Enough
It's Time To Rock
Baby You Know You Want Me
So Come Over And Rock With Me
Because Sweet Baby – It's Time To Rock

198. Making Love (AKA Bath Time Sex)

I-Ask-You – For a Date
You-Say-Maybe – Next-Time
I-Say – It's-Next-Time
You-Tell-Me – That-You-Have
To-Wash-Your-Hair – And
Soak-Your – Sexy-Body

I-Tell-You – I-Will-Wash
Your-Ass and Scrub-Your-Face
You-Laugh and Tell-Me – I'm-Dirty
That-I-Need to Soak – With-You
In-Your-Tub – For-Hours and Hours

(Chorus)
Making Love Is Fun
But Bath Time Sex Is Better
All You Have To Do Is
Drain Then Refill The Water
So You Can Keep On – Being Cleaner
While Having More – Bath Time Sex

Bubbles and Naked-Bodies
Shampoo and Steamy-Kisses
Moans – With-Nice-Wet – Splashes
We-Are-Both so Very-Dirty
That's-It-Baby – Wash-Me-Clean

(Chorus)
Making Love Is Fun
But Bath Time Sex Is Better
All You Have To Do Is
Drain Then Refill The Water
So You Can Keep On – Being Cleaner
While Having More – Bath Time Sex

(Fading Away)
Hey-Baby – I-Had a Great-Time
How-About – Next-Time-Baby
We-Wash-Ourselves – On-Your-Bed
So-We-Can – Make-Love – Without-Any-Waves

199. Rock And Roll Lovers

Like-Magic at First-Sight
They-Became – Hot-Lovers
That-Loved to Roll and Roll
The-Night-Away in Loving-Motion

Like-Magic – Once-Again
These-Hot-Lovers – Started-To – Like-To
Rock and Rock – Harder
Making-Them – Become-Rocking-Legends

(Chorus)
Let's Hear It For The
Rock And Roll Lovers
As The World Keeps Turning
They Keep On Burning – And
Rocking And Rolling
Like There Is No Tomorrow

People-Try – But it Does-No-Good
To-Separate – These-Magic-Lovers
Because – Their-Loving-Magic
Is-Filled-Up-With – Rock and Roll
We're of No-Concern

It's-Not-Their-Fault – It's-Magic
That-Has-Blessed – Their-Hearts
They-Found – Each-Other
Like a Whisper – On a Flame
That-Will-Burn – Strong and Bright
Until-They – Fade-Away and Die

(Chorus)
Let's Hear It For The
Rock And Roll Lovers
As The World Keeps Turning
They Keep On Burning – And
Rocking And Rolling
Like There Is No Tomorrow

200. Kiss Of Death

In-The-Dark of Night – Dressed in Black
She-Strolls – Free and Un-Loving
Waiting-On-Her – New-Prey
To-Come-Up to Her – Looking
For-Some-Hot-Lust – In-The-Dark of Night

She-Stops-Suddenly – So-Sweet
Smelling-Her – New-Fresh-Meal
Her-Body-Tingles – Evilly
With-Motions of Calmness
Seducing – This-Horny-Fool

(Chorus)
She Lets You Get Close
Her Scent Drives You Wild
While She Speaks So Soft
Words That Make You Surrender
All You Can Do Is – Stay Still
While She Gives You Her
Kiss Of Death – Her Kiss Of Death

She-Walks-Away – Licking-Red
Off-The-Tips of Her
Red – Dripping – Fingers
Singing – With-Moon-Beams
Dancing – With-Star-Shines

Loving-This-Dark-Night
That-She is Such a Beautiful
Mistress of Darkness – That
Loves-Making-Men-Bleed
To-Slate-Her – Taste-For-Blood

(Chorus)
She Lets You Get Close
Her Scent Drives You Wild
While She Speaks So Soft
Words That Make You Surrender
All You Can Do Is – Stay Still
While She Gives You Her
Kiss Of Death – Her Kiss Of Death

(Bonus)
Lady From Space (Sex Version) (347.)

I-Don't-Know – Her-Name
I-Can't-Understand – Her-Speech
And-I-Don't-Care – For
What-I'm-Looking-At
Is a Lady-From-Space

She-Has-Such a Fine – Purple and Pink
Sexy-Spaced-Out-Body – For-Me to Look-At
Get-Interested-In and About to Explore
As-She-Smiles – Her-Extra-Wide-Mouth
Showing-Me – Her-Extra-Long – Double-Tongues

(Chorus)
She's Not From Around Here
She's A Lady From Space
Out For A Weekend – Sex-Exploring Space
She's Not Interested In Love
She's Only Interested In Great Sex
So I Said Yes And She Space Sexed Me

I-Could-Be – Nice and Polite
Saying-I'm-Lucky – Being-Picked
By-Such a Fine – Space-Lady
But-That's-Not-Me – And-I-Know-It
By-Her-Eyes – That-She-Knows-It-To

She-Heard – Somewhere-Out in Space
That-Earth-Men – Can-Go and Go-Good
So-She-Brought – Along-With-Her
A-Large-Suitcase – Filled-Up-With
Space-Toys and Space-Oils
For-Us to Sample and Enjoy

(Chorus)
She's Not From Around Here
She's A Lady From Space
Out For A Weekend – Sex-Exploring Space
She's Not Interested In Love
She's Only Interested In Great Sex
So I Said Yes And She Space Sexed Me

76

Wow! – What a Night – I-Had-Last-Night
I'll-Never-Be – The-Same-Again
Earth-Women – Are-So-Very-Fine
But-Compared – To-My-Space-Lady

They-Are-Two – Arms-Too-Short
They-Don't-Have – That-Special-Scent
To-Drive-Me – Space-Sexually-Wild
Making-Me-Feel – Like-I'm the Greatest
Human-Man – That-Ever-Lived

(Chorus)
She's Not From Around Here
She's A Lady From Space
Out For A Weekend – Sex-Exploring Space
She's Not Interested In Love
She's Only Interested In Great Sex
So I Said Yes And She Space Sexed Me

(Chorus)
She's Not From Around Here
She's A Lady From Space
Out For A Weekend – Sex-Exploring Space
She's Not Interested In Love
She's Only Interested In Great Sex
So I Said Yes And She Space Sexed Me

(Bonus)
I Had A Lot Better (404.)

It's-Not – My-Fault
I-Tell-You – It's-Theirs
I-Know – What to Do
While-Making-Sex – And
I-Don't-Mind at All
Doing-Most of The-Work

But-At-The-Least – They-Could-Look
Alive – Instead of Giving – Me-Eyes
Saying – I-Can't-Believe-This
I-Think-I'm – Falling in Love

(Chorus)
Don't Cry Baby
As I Tell You
I Had A Lot Better
I'll Tell You What – Baby
If You Promise To Do Better
I'll Give You Another Chance

It-Gets-Old – Sometimes
Always – Finding – Ladies
That-Want to Fall-In-Love
Instead of Wanting to Have
A-Great-Time – Having-Sex
Waking-Up – On the Floor
All-Tired and Sexed-Out

(Chorus)
Don't Cry Baby
As I Tell You
I Had A Lot Better
I'll Tell You What – Baby
If You Promise To Do Better
I'll Give You Another Chance

Go-Ahead and Give-Me-Grief
For-Being a Selfish – Sexy-Stud
I-Don't-Give a Damn
'Cause-I-Get – Laid-All the Time
Be-Jealous – All-You-Want
Knowing – That-Your-Chance
Only-Comes-After
I-Already – Had-Them-First

(Chorus)
Don't Cry Baby
As I Tell You
I Had A Lot Better
I'll Tell You What – Baby
If You Promise To Do Better
I'll Give You Another Chance

(Demos) (Pages 79-84)

(Books Nine And Ten)

All My Love (Sunshine Dealer)

Sun Shining Love

Thunder Love

It's Your Fault (And You Know It)

Why Say No   –   When You Can Say Yes

All My Love (Sunshine Dealer) (Demo)

You-Must-Be a Sunshine-Dealer
Or-Work-Hand-In-Hand – With-The-Sun
For-You – Shine so Bright
That-You-Radiate – Your
Sweet-Shining-Beautiful-Love

I-Have-It so Great
Basking-In-It – Every-Single-Day
Feeling the Peace of Your-Love
I'm-So-Happy – Never a Sad-Thought
Going-Through – My-Mind

(Chorus)
All My Love
For You My Darling
So Thankful That You
Showed Me The True Meaning
Of What Love Is All About

You-Must-Be a Sunshine-Dealer
Or-Work-Hand-In-Hand – With-The-Sun
For-You – Shine so Bright
That-You-Radiate – Your
Sweet-Shining-Beautiful-Love

Even-When it's Cold – I-Never-Shiver
Because-All-I-Have-To-Do-Is
Scoot-Closer to Your – Sunshine-Love
Letting it Soak – Into-Me
As-I-Surrender – My-Soul – To-Our-Love

(Chorus)
All My Love
For You My Darling
So Thankful That You
Showed Me The True Meaning
Of What Love Is All About

Sun Shining Love (Demo)

I-Feel-Good and Ready
I-Don't-Want to Be-Late
'Cause-I-Got – Another-Hot-Date
With-This – Hot-Love-Lady

This-Lady – Has-Been-On – My-Mind
Ever-Since – I-Saw-Her – From-Behind
Bathing-Naked in The-Sun
My-Eyes – Could-Not-Look-Away
From-Her-Beautiful – Bare-Body

(Chorus)
Sun Shining Love
I Want You So Much
I'll Do Anything You Need
Just To Be Able To Enjoy Your
Sun Shining Love For Awhile

She-Looks-Me – In the Eyes
With-No-Fear in Them
Telling-Me to Look-Harder
Loving the Excitement – She-Brings
Knowing – I-Only-Want – Some-Lovin'

She's-In-Total-Control
Making-Me-Beg-Hard
Just to Keep – Touching-Her
'Cause – She's so Fine
And-She-Knows-It
Which is Very – Very-Good

(Chorus)
Sun Shining Love
I Want You So Much
I'll Do Anything You Need
Just To Be Able To Enjoy Your
Sun Shining Love For Awhile

Thunder Love (Demo)

Thunder – Loving – Ready
I-Take – The-Night
With-My-Giant-Love
Looking-For the Right-Ones
That-Love – Fine-Lovin'

I'm-The-One – Yes-I-Am
That-Can – Take-You-Higher
To the Height of Your-Desire
If-You-Want – This-Lovin' of Mine
All-You-Gotta-Do-Is – Join-In

(Chorus)
Thunder Love
Across The Sky
Great Souls Of Fire
We Burn With Desire
Thunder Love
Thunder Love With Me Baby

Where-You-Going – Sexy
I'm-Not-Done-With-You
I'm-Only – Half-Way-Through
Don't-Leave – These-Three
Ladies-All-Alone – Trying to Cope
With-My – Thunder-Love

That's-OK – Take-Your-Moment
I-Understand – Completely-Baby
Believe-Me – You're-Not the First
That-Couldn't – Take-All-My – Thunder-Loving

(Chorus)
Thunder Love
Across The Sky
Great Souls Of Fire
We Burn With Desire
Thunder Love
Thunder Love With Me Baby

It's Your Fault (And You Know It) (Demo)

Time-After-Time – You-Cheat
On-Me – Like-I-Don't
Give-You – Want-You-Want
It's so Sad – That-You

Make-Me – Do the Same
Getting-It-On – With the Hottest
Ladies-That-Know – How to Shake
Their-Asses – For-Sex

(Chorus)
It's Your Fault
And You Know It
You Cheat So Much
It's All I Can Do
To Keep Up With Your
Cheating Ways

You-Tell-Me – You-Have a
Free-Living – Life-Style
That-One-Man – Can't-Hang
With-Your-Hot – Sexual-Ways
I-Tell-You to Stick-Around
For 15 Minutes

I-Will – Rock-You
Like-You – Need to Be-Rocked
'Cause-Baby – I've-Got a Blessing
My-Thunder-Love – My-Third-Leg
That-Out-Shines the Mightiest
Like a Tree – To a Stick

(Chorus)
It's Your Fault
And You Know It
You Cheat So Much
It's All I Can Do
To Keep Up With Your
Cheating Ways

Why Say No – When You Can Say Yes (Demo)

I-Unzip – My-Pants
You-Say – You-Want to Wait
I-Pull-Down – My-Pants
You-Smile and Flush
You-Can't – Help-Yourself

I'm a Man – That-Knows
How to Make a Woman
Regret – Her – Decision
With a Smile – On-Her-Lips
So-Baby – How-About-This

(Chorus)
Why Say No
When You Can Say Yes
Don't Hesitate Baby
Let's Rock And Roll
On The Floor – Like People
That Love To Have Sex

You-Learn-Fast-Baby
After-We're-Done – You-Wait
Holding-Your-Breath so Impatiently
For-My-15-Minutes – To-Be-Over-With
I-Give-You a Kiss – Then-I-Tell-You
To-Get-Me a Cold-Beer

You-Come-Back – With-My-Beer in Hand
Thinking too Much – About-Should-You-Again
With a Man – That-You-Just-Met
A-Few – Hours-Ago
I-Recognize – Your-Look and Say
Baby – How-About-This

(Chorus)
Why Say No
When You Can Say Yes
Don't Hesitate Baby
Let's Rock And Roll
On The Floor – Like People
That Love To Have Sex

84

I May Never Be Able To Go Home Again (Pages 85-87)

My Love,

(Week One) I have finally made it here, life is hard in this new world, every day it seems like someone is in the ready to take my feet out from underneath me. I try my best to stay positive. The memory of your warm face helps me get through the cold, alone, without you nights, that are starting to take their toll on my body. With no money for shelter, myself and a few friends that I have made, get together and band as one, doing what it takes to keep ourselves alive. It is hard, some of us have not survived enough to stay alive. Three men so far have frozen to death out in the cold of the unforgiving nights that gives no calm, only a heed that many more of them will come for us to take our lives unless we are strong and lucky enough to live through until the first day of spring comes to us like a blessing from this very close but not our mother Earth.

(Week Two) Things have changed, I miss Earth so much. The voyage out here was the best thing about my trip, the stay and make it plan I had. I'm not too proud to admit when I make a mistake, this is not my or anybody else's mistake that we came. We were lied to, we are slaves to the disgusting filth that has taken over like power hungry monsters with no conscience, only power, money, power the mighty with their armies to keep all those that are individuals down, working for them for nothing but for some food and clothes, no toiletries, no respect, no dignity for a person's rights.

(Week Fifty) Ten of us has escaped, trying to live on our own, I am the strongest and the leader, I eat first, I protect them and myself. No way can I live my life on this planet that has no soul and only blood and death. I sneak up and take a look, I have almost discovered the way to fly a small ship by watching very close without ever being seen as the soldiers of the corrupted, drink themselves to happiness, while wiping our blood from their hands without a thought of mercy inside themselves. What is this new world? It is ten times the worst of Earth. I am coming home a criminal for not wanting to be a slave. I don't give a damn, I am a good and decent man that only wants my promised wealth from working hard, making the land I own ready to produce large amounts of food for Earth. The large amounts of food is very true, for we are worked to death and beaten for taking too long doing what we are told to do. Everybody hates this, everybody hates everybody. They blame themselves and blame everyone. Hate reigns supreme when you have nothing and someone else does.

(Week Seventy Five) I pick tomorrow's daylight to be the time I am coming home to you. I can not wait 'til I can see your face and body. I will hold you, and I will make love to you many times, for I have been without just like I know you have my love. I cannot wait to give you back the man that you love, my love. I have changed, I'm very lean and mean looking but I still have my love for you as a piece of luck with me always until I can replace it with you once again. I hope your life has been good and safe, I know you have written me wondering and worrying that I have not written you first. I have never received any mail, no one has, it all gets burned. These few pieces of paper that I am writing you with is all that I can obtain. It may seem foolish to do this when I will be able to see you in a year.

Susses, I did it, I stole a ship right out from under them and they didn't even come after me. I escaped without an accident and am on my way to you and Earth my love. I thought of something my love, something that I am going to do when I see you. I am going to sing this song to you I hope you love it as much as I love you.

Take Me In Your Arms

Alone in Space – Is so Lonely
No-Ships – Ever-Cross-My-Path
I'm the Man – In the Bottle
That-Has-Control – Over-It

I-Speed – Towards-You – With-Love
Inside-My-Heart for You – My-Love
I-Can-Not-Help – Myself-From-Shaking
From the Pain – I-Had to Endure
I'm-Scarred – Torn and Very-Worn
I-Need-Your-Love to Help-Me-Heal

(Chorus)
Take Me In Your Arms
Give Me Your Love
I Need It So Very Bad
Take Me In Your Arms
My Body Craves To Be Touched
By Your Body That I Worship
Take Me In Your Arms
I Can Feel You In My Head
Let Me Do As I Will – My Love

(One Year Later) To those that want to know what happened to me after I got back to Earth. Well I am a criminal that is locked up. I landed, called my love, she sounded so nervous and happy. We met, I gave her a hug then a kiss, she kissed me and told me that she was sorry. She had no choice, she had to think of the child that belongs to me, that I did not know that I had. Emotions erupted inside me as police officers came in with guns showing, ready to kill me if I moved. I looked up at my love with a boot on my neck and guns in my face and told her that I loved her. My love told me that she loved me too but her life is outside of jail, so she hopes that I understand that she had to go on with her life and find a man that loved her and took care of her.

The police officers held me still so I could hear every sad word that was breaking my heart, then they laughed out loud telling me that my woman was on the market now and some of them gave her their numbers, some of them got her number. I could not believe her betrayal. To everyone in this room I was not even a person at all, I was just something that needed to be locked away. I did not even try to tell these jackals of the oppression that I had to endure. On my date in court, I told my tale, the judge looked at me and gave me five extra years for perjury on top of the twenty years for my other crimes, too many to tell and all are lies and crap except for the ship I stole, but of course I had no choice.

I'm waiting twenty five years now trying to find a way to escape the Hell that I am living with, I do not see it happening any time soon. I wish I could go back in time and not quit my job and travel in space to another planet to make my fortune come true. I had enough with my old life, I loved and I was loved, I was liked by many friends that sent me off with a great big party, not one of them came to see me or to speak in my name for the good person that I am. Goodbye to whom ever wanted to know.

(Five Years later) One day I am in Hell, the next day I am outside in the sun, free and about to make a lot of money. The judge on the take, paid off by the rulers of the other Planet, was caught with his bank account with too much money in it, when some good people went searching when others like myself found their way back to Earth. My love wants me back, her child is not even mine, I laugh and tell her goodbye. "I may never be able to go home again" but I am now lying on a beach, on a island without a care in the world, loving this beautiful sunny day, trying to forget my pains by having beautiful women taking care of me with their lovely suntanned bodies.

Love Questions

I – Love – You
You – Love – Me
Do-I-Love-You
Do-You-Love-Me

Love-Questions – That-Get-Answered
Love-Questions – That-Never-Get-Answered
Love-Is-Love – It-Is-What-It-Is
Love-Is-Heart-Warming – Love-Is-Heart-Breaking

I'm-Happy – She's-The-One
I'm-Happy – He's-The-One
I'm-Happy – Is-She-The-One
I'm-Happy – Is-He-The-One

Love-Questions – That-Get-Answered
Love-Questions – That-Never-Get-Answered
Love-Is-Love – It-Is-What-It-Is
Love-Is-Heart-Warming – Love-Is-Heart-Breaking

I-Love-Her – Today
I-Love-Him – Today
Will-I-Love-Her – Tomorrow
Will-I-Love-Him – Tomorrow

Love-Questions – That-Get-Answered
Love-Questions – That-Never-Get-Answered
Love-Is-Love – It-Is-What-It-Is
Love-Is-Heart-Warming – Love-Is-Heart-Breaking

She-Loved-Me – From-The-Start
He-Loved-Me – From-The-Start
Will-She-Love-Me – 'Til-The-End
Will-He-Love-Me – 'Til-The-End

Love-Questions – That-Get-Answered
Love-Questions – That-Never-Get-Answered
Love-Is-Love – It-Is-What-It-Is
Love-Is-Heart-Warming – Love-Is-Heart-Breaking

The Yellow With A Pink Heart Balloon

Took a Drive to Nowhere
On the Side of The-Road
Tied to a Slow-Down or Die-Sign
Was a Yellow-Balloon
With A Pink-Heart – In the Center of It

Amazing to My-Eyes – I-Felt-Beauty
Inside-My-Mind – Inside-My-Heart
Time-Slowed-Down as Heavy
Saturated – My – Soul
Looking at It – Through-My-Mirrors

I've-Stopped – Shaking-With-Fear
I'm-Alone – No-One-Loves-Me
The-World is So-Cold
I-Have-Nothing – I-Have-My-Self
It's-Time to Warm-My-Soul

Walk-Away – Leave-My-Car
Leave-My-Life – Behind
My-Life-Has-Stopped
I'm-Myself – I-Can't-Change
Now-I'm-New – No-More the Same

Will-I-Now – Find-Love
Yes – I – Will
One-Fresh-Chance is All-I-Get
It's-All – I-Need
Love – Love – Love
You-Are-My – Very-Soon to Be

One-Year and One-Day – Later
I'm-In-Love – With-My-Lover
Our-Love is Warm – Soft and Fine

The-Yellow – With a Pink-Heart-Balloon
Is-Placed – On-Our-Wall
With a Reminder – Love-Rules
When-You-Have a Broken-Heart
It-Even-Rules – When-You-Don't
Feel-It – In-Your-Heart

Give It To Me Baby (523.) (New Cover Bonus)

I-Walk-With-You – As-You
Give-Me – Your-Half-Love
You-Need-Me to Be – Your-Man
But-You – Don't-Want to Be – My-Lady

Sex-With-Me is So-Perfect
I-Know-My-Way – Around a Lady
Keeping-You – Flushed and Panting
Is-All – That-You – Want-From-Me
Baby – I-Don't-Mind at All

(Chorus)
I Look Into Your Eyes And Say
You're So Fine – Give It To Me Baby
You Know I Lust You So Much
Come On Baby – Give It To Me Baby

Shaking – Trying-Not to Touch-Me
You-Look at Me and I-Know
It-Was-Fun – But it's Over
Gentleman-While – Kissing-Your-Hand
It's-Alright-Baby – It's-Okay-Baby
Time for Us – Not to Be – As-One

(Chorus)
I Look Into Your Eyes And Say
You're So Fine – Give It To Me Baby
You Know I Lust You So Much
Come On Baby – Give It To Me Baby

On the Floor – Holding-On to My-Leg
Before-I-Can – Make-It to The-Door
Trying to Kiss-Me – Back-Into-Your-Bed
Begging-Always – Does-Some-Good
As-I-Tell-You to Lay-Down
As-I-get-My – Next-'Til-Tomorrow

(Chorus)
I Look Into Your Eyes And Say
You're So Fine – Give It To Me Baby
You Know I Lust You So Much
Come On Baby – Give It To Me Baby

Sex Is The Answer (559.) (New Cover Bonus)

He-Wants-Her – She-Wants-Him
They-Smile-Real-Nice
While-Putting-Food in Their-Mouths

Conversation is Polite – Not-Going-Anywhere
While-Both of Them – Can't-Hold-Still in Their-Chairs

(Chorus)
Sex Is The Answer
When You Don't Have
Anything To Talk About
Sex Is The Answer
It's Better Than Just
Staring At Each Other

You-Use to Date-Her-Friend
Now-You-Want to Date-Her
She-Always-Smiled – Real-Nice
While-Staring at Your-Pants

Walk-Over-Real-Cool – Remembering too Late
You-Don't – Remember-Her-Name
Just-Play it Cool – Talk-About-Sex

(Chorus)
Sex Is The Answer
When You Don't Have
Anything To Talk About
Sex Is The Answer
It's Better Than Just
Staring At Each Other

He-Don't-Like-Her – He-Likes-Her-Body
She-Don't-Like-Him – She-likes-His-Body

Always the Same – Too-Much-Thinking
Shut-Up – Go-Hump-Already
Who-Cares if You-Like – Each-Other or Not
What's-Most-Important in Life
Is to Find-Someone – That-Turns-You-On

(Repeat Chorus)
91